bedeviled

LOVE STRUCK

FOUNTAIN___ ___ LIBRARY DISTRICT
3__ __st Briarcliff Road
Bolingbrook, IL 60440-2894
(630) 759-2102

by Shani Petroff
Grosset & Dunlap

An Imprint of Penguin Group (USA) Inc.

GROSSET & DUNLAP
Published by the Penguin Group
Penguin Group (USA) Inc., 375 Hudson Street, New York, New York 10014, USA
Penguin Group (Canada), 90 Eglinton Avenue East, Suite 700, Toronto, Ontario
M4P 2Y3, Canada (a division of Pearson Penguin Canada Inc.)
Penguin Books Ltd., 80 Strand, London WC2R 0RL, England
Penguin Group Ireland, 25 St. Stephen's Green, Dublin 2, Ireland
(a division of Penguin Books Ltd.)
Penguin Group (Australia), 250 Camberwell Road, Camberwell, Victoria 3124,
Australia (a division of Pearson Australia Group Pty. Ltd.)
Penguin Books India Pvt. Ltd., 11 Community Centre,
Panchsheel Park, New Delhi—110 017, India
Penguin Group (NZ), 67 Apollo Drive, Rosedale, North Shore 0632, New Zealand
(a division of Pearson New Zealand Ltd.)
Penguin Books (South Africa) (Pty.) Ltd., 24 Sturdee Avenue, Rosebank,
Johannesburg 2196, South Africa
Penguin Books Ltd., Registered Offices: 80 Strand, London WC2R 0RL, England

The publisher does not have any control over and does not assume any
responsibility for author or third-party websites or their content.

If you purchased this book without a cover, you should be aware that this
book is stolen property. It was reported as "unsold and destroyed" to the publisher,
and neither the author nor the publisher has received any payment for this
"stripped book."

The scanning, uploading, and distribution of this book via the Internet or via any
other means without the permission of the publisher is illegal and punishable by
law. Please purchase only authorized electronic editions and do not participate
in or encourage electronic piracy of copyrighted materials. Your support of the
author's rights is appreciated.

Text copyright © 2010 by Shani Petroff. Cover image © 2010 by Penguin Group
(USA) Inc. All rights reserved. Published by Grosset & Dunlap, a division of
Penguin Young Readers Group, 345 Hudson Street, New York, New York 10014.
GROSSET & DUNLAP is a trademark of Penguin Group (USA) Inc.
Printed in the U.S.A.

Cover illustration by J. David McKenney.

Library of Congress Cataloging-in-Publication Data is available.

ISBN 978-0-448-45114-5   10 9 8 7 6 5 4 3 2 1

To Andrea S. Petroff,
The sister I always wanted and finally have.
You're a wonderful addition to the family.
Love you.

A lot of people helped me bring this book to life. I'd like to thank:

My wonderful family and friends for all of their love and support.

With special mention to my mother, Marilyn, who has gone above
and beyond for me. My brother, Jordan, who has acted as the
perfect sounding board, consultant, and friend.
And my father, Robert, who will always live in my heart.

My agent, Jodi Reamer, for her advice and guidance. As well
as Alec Shane and the rest of Writers House.

J. David McKenney for his fabulous cover illustration.

And, of course, the people at Penguin. To Francesco Sedita and
Bonnie Bader for believing in both the series and me. To Judy Goldschmidt
for her support through this whole process, her editorial input, and for
making Bedeviled everything it can be. And to everyone who has worked
on the series and helped make it a reality.

And of course the booksellers, librarians, and readers who have spread
the word about Bedeviled and who love Angel just as much as I do.

Thank you all!

chapter

1

"Marc is looking at you," I whispered to my BFF Gabi Gottlieb, hiding my mouth with my burger.

Gabi glanced over to the popular table and then back at her Tofurky sandwich. "Probably wondering why he ever hung around with a dork like me," she mumbled.

"That's not true," I protested.

She gave me a long, hard stare as I tried to think of something brilliant to say that would cheer her up. But as I studied the intricacies of the ketchup packet lying on my tray, nothing sprang to mind. Nothing other than that I should never have brought up Marc Greyson to begin with.

Gabi had a big crush on Marc. And for a brief second not too long ago, it looked like he had liked her, too. Only his feelings weren't real.

They were the result of powers. Mine, to be exact.

Angel Garrett, daughter of the devil, struck again. I'd accidentally made all of Gabi's wishes come true. And that included having Marc like her. As well as Cole Daniels. And who is Cole Daniels, you ask? Cole Daniels is my boyfriend.

It was awful, to say the least. For me, anyway.

Everything eventually got back to normal—including Marc's feelings. But now Gabi was stuck crushing on a guy that only saw her as co-captain of the nerd herd. Not exactly the image she was going for.

"Once Marc *really* gets to know you he'll want to go out with you," I said, dropping my burger.

Gabi glanced back at Marc. "No way. Have you seen him? He can get any girl he wants. He'd never pick me." She let out a sigh.

"You don't know that," I said. "He could surprise you."

"Soooo." Gabi tugged at her braid. "Any more Lou sightings?" she asked, changing the subject from one she didn't like discussing to one I hated even thinking about.

"No, thank goodness."

My father, better known as Lou Cipher, aka Lucifer, and I were not exactly on speaking terms. I found out he hadn't given up all of his evil tricks. He'd made excuses for why and said it wasn't his fault, but I wasn't buying it. I told him I would let him into my life if he stopped granting wishes in exchange for people's souls. And until I knew for sure that he had changed for good, we were done. In the meantime, I asked him to stay away. So far it had been a week, and no surprise visits. My fingers were crossed that it would stay that way.

I could tell Gabi wanted to say something, but she shut her mouth. It was a good thing, too, because I knew what she was going to say. That I was being too hard on Lou. We'd had the same conversation about a dozen times and it always got me riled up. I wasn't looking for a fight. Especially not with Gabi.

The whole wish-granting/Cole-stealing fiasco had put a temporary strain on our friendship. We'd gotten past it, but I wanted to stay on neutral territory for a while. So I switched to something we could both agree on.

"I cannot wait to meet Lance tomorrow!"

Lance Gold was the hottest actor on the planet. That's not even an exaggeration. He won the title eight weeks in a row in *Teen Wow* magazine. And his reign was probably going to last forever.

"If we can even get close to him. The mall is going to be swamped."

"That's where my special gift comes in," I said, wiggling my fingers.

"Angel . . . ," Gabi said in her control-freak mother's reprimanding voice.

"What? I'm not going to do anything stupid. I learned my lesson. No advanced powers for me. I'll stick to the basics." The only powers I had under control were moving objects (including people) and stopping them in their tracks. Not as cool as turning green beans into hundred-dollar bills, but it did have its advantages. "I can just part the crowd and we can walk right on up to Lance. Simple."

"Nothing with you and your powers is ever simple," she said, popping a soy apple crisp into her mouth.

"You'll see," I assured her. "But it doesn't even matter. I won't need to use my powers. The whole reason Lance is here is because of you. It would be just plain cruel if they didn't give you a personal introduction."

Lance had gotten caught up in Gabi's whole wish-making disaster. She was starring in her own reality TV show, and he was supposed to do a photo shoot with her. It never ended up happening because the wishes got reversed. But since Lance was already scheduled to come to Pennsylvania, his producer had turned the visit into a mall appearance set for tomorrow. Everyone was going to be there.

"Are you kidding? Personal introduction?" Gabi practically shrieked. "Without the show, I'm a nobody. I'm not getting any closer to Lance Gold than anyone else at the mall."

She needed more faith. "Just wait," I assured her. "You'll see."

Just then I saw Cole approaching our table. "See what?" he asked.

"We're just talking about tomorrow," I said, covering my stomach with my arm. It always did this wild hula dance whenever Cole was around. I knew it wasn't visible to the human eye. But still, I wasn't taking any chances.

"It's okay that I come with you guys, right?" he asked looking from me to Gabi and then quickly back to me.

"Of course," I said.

Gabi nodded her head slightly. "Yeah," she said quietly.

"Cool." Cole was only allowing himself to look at Gabi out of the corner of his eye.

Things had been kind of weird between the two of them since she accidentally made him want to date her. Cole doesn't know anything about powers. So he thinks he's to blame for momentarily dumping me for my best friend. He's apologized a zillion times and begged me to forgive him. And I did. I had to. He never would have done it if I hadn't given Gabi wish-making capabilities.

"Do you want to sit?" I asked Cole.

"That's okay. I should be getting back to my table in a minute." Cole hadn't sat with us all week. I think he was embarrassed to be around Gabi because of the whole crush thing. But I needed him to get over it. I couldn't go through life with my boyfriend being all awkward around my best friend. I wanted us to be able to have fun together—not feel like we were stuck in detention.

"We finally finish up *Romeo and Juliet* next week," I said, trying to break the tension.

"About time," Cole and Gabi said at the exact same time.

That got them to laugh, and they smiled at each other.

I was so relieved, I wasn't even jealous that they made eye contact. "I can't wait until we get to write our own plays and then act them out," Gabi said.

That was going to be our next English assignment. I wasn't as excited about it as she was, but it sure beat Shakespeare. "Mrs. Torin better let us pick our own groups," I said.

"She probably will." Gabi clapped her hands together. "We can even add some songs. Make it a musical."

Gabi had a great voice.

"I could help write the music," Cole said, actually getting excited. "I've been working on some things."

Whoa! I did not know Cole wrote songs. Sure, he was way into music. But I thought he just liked to listen.

"Like that piece you played for Jason after Hebrew School?" she asked.

Hmmm . . . Gabi, on the other hand, knew all about it.

"Yeah," he said, kicking a napkin on the floor. "I didn't know you heard that."

"It was really good," she said.

He gave her one of his amazing, lopsided smiles.

Okay. Now I was starting to get a little uncomfortable.

She smiled back.

Enough was enough.

It was definitely time to find Gabi a boyfriend.

Her *own* boyfriend.

chapter

2

"Forgot to tell Cole something," I said to Gabi as we headed to French. "Meet you in class." I ran off before she could answer.

Okay, it was a teeny lie. I hadn't forgotten anything. I just needed a second alone with Cole so I could talk to him. I wanted him to convince Marc to ask Gabi out. Gabi would have chained me to the trophy case and stuffed my mouth with a sweaty sock before letting me go through with this plan.

"I need you to do me a favor," I said, meeting Cole at his locker.

"Sure, what's up?" he asked.

When I told him what I wanted, his face got all twisty. "I don't know," he said.

My stomach felt like someone, someone like Cole, was stabbing it with toothpicks. Didn't he want Gabi to have a boyfriend? Or did he secretly want her to be alone so he could have a chance with her? I pinched my arm. I was being stupid. Cole liked me. "Why not?" I asked, before I could come up with any other scary scenarios.

"Just don't think it will work. They're so different. He's popular and she's—," Cole stopped himself.

But I wasn't letting him off that easy. I crossed my arms over my chest. "She's what?"

Cole studied his locker, almost like he was debating shutting himself inside instead of finishing the conversation with me. He shrugged his shoulders. "They're just from different groups."

Bad answer.

"We're from different groups and we go out," I said, staring him down.

"That's different," he said.

But it really wasn't. Cole was super-popular. And I was as big an outcast as Gabi. Maybe even a bigger one. "Yeah, how?" I asked. The stabs to my stomach were getting stronger.

"It just is," he said.

My whole body clenched. "No, it's not. So I guess this means you don't like to be seen with me, either? Am I too embarrassing for you?" Okay, I know that wasn't completely fair, but I was angry.

"No, that's not what I meant. It's just, Marc is different. He's more into what people think."

"Whatever, Cole," I said and turned around. "I'll ask him myself." Marc and I were not exactly buddies. Not even close. But I was going to talk to him, anyway. To help out Gabi. That was the kind of friend I was. Unlike some people . . .

"Wait." Cole let out a deep breath. "I'm sorry. Don't be mad at me. I'll talk to him."

"Yeah?" I asked.

"Yeah," Cole said.

Now was that so hard? Why couldn't he have just agreed to begin with? "Let's do it now," I suggested.

For a second Cole looked like he was going to say something, but he just closed his mouth and walked over to Marc, who was getting books out of his locker.

I held back my smile.

"Hey," Cole said as he stood in front of Marc. I hovered behind him.

"Hey," Marc answered, searching his locker. It was like mine—a total disaster zone.

"Hitting the mall tomorrow?" Cole asked.

"Yeah, I think everyone is," Marc said.

I gave Cole a nudge. The bell was going to ring any

minute. He needed to speed up his pitch.

"Well, Angel and I are going. And Gabi, too. You should come with us."

"Maybe," Marc said, still rummaging through his locker.

"Cool," Cole responded.

Cool? It wasn't cool. A maybe was halfway to no. It stunk. It was time for me to step in. "You know, Gabi is pretty amazing. Not only is she killer smart, but she's so much fun. You used to like her, right?" There was no time for subtlety. "I don't blame you. She is the prettiest girl in the whole eighth grade. How could you not?"

Both Marc and Cole were looking at me like I was nuts. Like a windup doll that just kept going and going and going even when no one wanted to play with it anymore. But I didn't care. I was on a mission.

"Looking for your homework?" I went on. There really was no stopping me. "If you can't find it, you should just ask Gabi. She's great at homework. I'm sure she'd be happy to help you. She's a whiz. She's good at everything. Don't you think?"

This time it was Cole's turn to nudge me.

Fine. Maybe I wasn't handling this the best possible way, but I was on a time limit. The bell was going to ring.

Marc didn't say a word.

"Well," I said, "can't wait to see you at the mall tomorrow. I know Gabi can't, either." She would have killed me if she knew what I was up to.

"Gabi?" Courtney Lourde said, walking over to us.

Figured. She had a knack for butting her nose in at the worst possible times. At least her little followers, Jaydin and Lana, weren't with her.

"Marc is going to be hanging out with *me* and *my* friends," she said, flipping her long, blond hair over her shoulder.

Gabi and I definitely didn't fall into that category.

"You're welcome to join us, too, Cole," she said, resting her hand on his arm.

"I'm going with Angel," Cole said, acting like he didn't notice what Courtney was doing.

"Too bad. If you decide to ditch Double-A—or is it Double-D now?" (She calls me Double-A because that's my bra size. But when I accidentally used my powers to turn my nonexistent chest into monster boobs, I was Double-D for a minute.) "Either way, if you change your mind, Cole, let me know."

Her hand was still on his arm.

I bet her boyfriend, D.L. Helper, would have loved that as much as I did.

The bell rang and Courtney turned her attention to

Marc. "Let's go before we're late."

He didn't even say good-bye to me—or Cole. He just followed Courtney like an obedient little puppy dog. No way was I going to accomplish anything with Courtney in the picture.

"What happened to *me* talking to Marc?" Cole asked when they were out of earshot.

"I got a little carried away."

"A little?!"

"I know! Did I blow it completely?"

The sound of the late bell saved Cole from answering. But I knew what he would have said. I messed up. Again.

I didn't even need to use my powers this time.

chapter

3

"We are about to meet Lance Gold!" I was just short of shouting as we walked through the mall. "This is so cool."

"It's not that big a deal," Cole said as he held my hand a little tighter. "He's just an actor."

I wasn't positive, but I thought I detected a little jealousy in Cole's tone. It was better when he was the one all nervous over nothing than when it was me.

"*Just* an actor. Are you nuts?" Gabi asked, throwing her hands into the air. "He's so much more than that. Not only can he act, but he can sing, play the drums, hit a fastball, and rock climb." She clearly had his *Teen Wow* bio memorized. "Plus," she went on, "he does tons of charity work. He's always helping people. Last week alone he raised tens of thousands of dollars for the Heart Association and did the Walk for the Cure race. He's even nice to his enemies. The other day, he made his limo pull over to help some paparazzi guy who had fallen off his bike. Most stars would have just left the guy there. But not Lance. He checked to make sure the photographer was okay and even posed for a picture."

"A regular saint," Cole said.

"Aww, come on," Gabi said. "You wouldn't be here if you didn't want to meet him, too."

"I just came for Angel," he said. But he wasn't fooling either one of us. We both knew he was excited to meet Lance. After all, wasn't he the same guy who wanted his (and my) favorite band, Mara's Daughters, to play at his Bar Mitzvah? The same guy who snuck peeks at my magazines when he thought I wasn't looking? He was just as—okay, *almost* as—celebrity obsessed as Gabi and me.

We weren't the only ones. The mall was packed. I had never seen it this busy. Not even the day after Thanksgiving.

"Let's try to get closer," Gabi said, grabbing my free hand and pulling me toward the stage area. The three of us squirmed through the crowd. It was so tight, we got pressed up between strangers. At one point, the back of one guy's sweaty T-shirt rubbed up against my face, I got an elbow to the side, and some tall girl's stinky armpit was pressing up against my nose—all within moments of one another.

"Watch it," some guy said as I smashed right into him.

"Sorry." I didn't mean to hit him, but I didn't really avoid him, either. My new strategy for the event? Face down, forge ahead, and anyone that got in my way would get head-butted.

"Angel?" the guy I bumped into asked.

I looked up. "D.L.? Didn't expect to see you here."

"Courtney dragged me," he said, letting out a deep breath.

"Know the feeling," Cole said. I didn't correct him. If he wanted to tell people the only reason he was there was because of me, I had no problem with it. I actually liked it. My boyfriend didn't care if people—even the popular ones—knew he did things just to make me happy.

"Aren't you going the wrong way?" Gabi asked D.L. "The stage is that way." She pointed to the direction he'd just come from.

"I'm over it. Courtney made us all get here three hours ago just to hear the guy sing. He's an actor. What does he know about music?"

"A lot," Gabi answered. "He's singing in his next movie, and he's planning on releasing his own CD. He can do everything. He's incredible."

"Whatever," D.L. mumbled. "I'm done waiting. I'm gonna go get a piece of pizza," he said. "Reid and everyone are over there," he told Cole and nodded his head behind him.

Reid was Cole's best friend. "Thanks," Cole said.

"Good luck getting there," D.L. said and then fought his way against the crowd.

I used to think he was just as awful as Courtney, but lately he had been acting a lot nicer. I was beginning to think he wasn't so bad—well, except for his taste in girlfriends.

"Let's go," Cole said. "I see Reid. He's not too far away." Gabi and I just stood there. Because while I didn't have any real issues with Reid, his girlfriend, Lana Perkins, was another story. She was one of Courtney's best friends. And spending the afternoon around her and Courtney was not something Gabi or I wanted to do. But I didn't want to tell Cole he couldn't hang out with his friends, either. That wasn't fair.

"Come on," Cole said again, this time leading the way. He squeezed my hand. "Don't worry about Courtney. She's all talk. She won't care if you're there.

Besides, someone else might be over there, too."

He mouthed the name Marc. But he was not exactly discreet. Gabi caught the whole thing.

"You told him I liked Marc!" she whispered as we made our way toward Courtney and Co.

"Not exactly . . . kind of . . . okay, yes." I caved as she stared me down. "But only because they're friends," I whispered back. "I wanted to know if he thought Marc would go out with you."

"And?" she asked.

Her voice sounded so excited. I didn't want to be the one to bring her down, so I fudged the truth. A lot. "He thinks you guys would be awesome together."

"Really?" she asked.

"Really," I echoed. Gabi looked like she was going to combust with happiness.

"Hey," Cole said as we approached his friends.

A couple of them called out his name and Reid even fist-bumped him. For a whole second I thought everything was going to be fine. That Courtney and I could be within a small radius of each other without insults flying. That we could ignore each other and go on with our lives. But who was I kidding? It was Courtney Lourde we were talking about, and she took her mean-girl status seriously.

"Well, look who's here," Courtney said in her singsong voice. "Cole and his community service projects."

"Courtney!" Cole warned.

"What?" she asked, opening her eyes superwide and trying to look all innocent.

"Lay off," he said. I liked that he was coming to my defense.

"Sorry," she said, giving him an almost angelic smile. "But I just don't understand why you like her. Is she blackmailing you? Offering you money to hang out? Did she pull some elaborate trick?"

"Enough," Cole said. "You're not funny."

She ignored him. "Or maybe she just pleaded with you. She's good at that. Right, Marc?" Courtney giggled. I felt my blood turn to ice water. I actually had goose bumps. I knew where this was going.

"You'll never guess what I saw yesterday," Courtney announced to everyone around her. "Double-A begging Marc to hang out with Gabi. She kept going on and on, trying to make it sound like Gabi was actually normal. It was so pathetic, *I* was almost embarrassed for her."

I could feel Gabi's eyes on me, but I didn't dare look up.

"Like Marc would want to go out with the school joke," Courtney said. "Would you, Marc?"

This time she actually waited for him to answer.

He snorted. "No way, would never happen."

I snuck a look at Gabi. She was gripping her braid hard. She didn't blush the way I did—I made stop signs look pale. But I could tell she was embarrassed and angry. Livid, actually.

"Hey," Courtney said, her voice perking up. "I saw Max a couple of minutes ago stalking the stage." Max Richardson was Goode Middle School's other unofficial human target. Courtney treated him like toe fungus. "Now there's a guy for you, Gabi. It'll be perfect—if you can tear him away from Angel. You guys can be 'class couple.' I can see the yearbook picture now. Only people might get confused and think it's an ad for the circus freak show. The giant and the world's ugliest woman."

She laughed at her own stupid joke. And she wasn't the only one. Marc did, too.

I felt awful. How could I have gotten Gabi's hopes up about such a creep!? Who needed Marc? If he was going to join in on the Gabi bashing, he didn't deserve her.

Gabi needed somebody better. Somebody nice.

Somebody who didn't care what the stupid A-list at Goode Middle School thought. Somebody who'd make them all jealous. Somebody who was an A-lister in their own right. A real one.

And I knew just the person.

chapter

4

Lance Gold.

I was going to fix up Gabi with everyone's favorite teen idol. She'd show them all. This was no longer about playing matchmaker to make sure Gabi didn't fall for Cole. This was about something way bigger: protecting my best friend. Courtney and Co. didn't have the right to make her feel like a deflated kickball. Especially because of something *I* did.

My new plan was perfect. Not only would Gabi get an awesome boyfriend, but no one would ever make fun of her again. They'd be too busy trying to get on her good side so they could get autographs and invitations to celebrity parties.

"I need to go to the bathroom," I told Gabi. "Come with me."

Gabi nodded. I could tell she was mad at me, but

she didn't want to be around Courtney any more than I did.

"We'll be right back," I told Cole.

"'K," he said. "Sorry about this."

"Not your fault." And it wasn't. I gave Courtney a quick glare.

"I'll talk to her again," he said, following my gaze.

"Thanks, but don't bother. I can handle her." While I appreciated Cole's offer, I couldn't take him up on it. Having him talk to Courtney would only make things worse. She'd just torture us more but make sure not to do it in front of Cole. And I'd rather him see what a horrible person his "friend" was firsthand.

I led Gabi through the crowd.

"How could you do that to me?" Gabi said through gritted teeth once we were away from Courtney. "It was bad enough you told Cole about my crush—but *Marc*? What were you thinking?"

"I was just trying to help."

"Well, you didn't."

"I'm sorry," I said quietly. And I was. She'd see. I was going to make it up to her big time.

The tone of her voice lightened a little. "Just stay out of my love life from now on."

I didn't say anything. I couldn't. Not without lying.

And this was for her own good. By the time the day was over, Gabi would be showering me with gifts for butting in. I was sure of it. After all, she'd be on the path to becoming Mrs. Lance Gold.

"Wait," she said. "Where are we going? This isn't the way to the bathroom."

"Shortcut," I told her.

No reason to tell her what I had in mind until the last possible moment. That way she couldn't back out.

"This is *not* a shortcut," she said as we inched closer to the fake wall that separated the crowd from Lance's backstage area. "Where are you taking me?"

"Trust me," I said.

"Angel, what's going on?" she demanded. "I'm not moving another inch until you tell me."

"Okay," I said. "That"—I pointed to the side entrance of the old Clothes Therapy store—"is what's going on." The store had moved locations, and the mall was using the empty store as a backstage area for its guest star. "Our chance to meet Lance."

There was a stage built in front of the main entrance with a curtain where the door was supposed to be. So there was no way of getting to Lance that way. Not unless we wanted a mob of people to try to stop us. But with the exception of two guards, there was no one standing by the side entrance. We just had to slip in there and we were golden.

"Are you nuts? We can't break into the store!" she said.

"It's not breaking in," I clarified. "It's actually more like trespassing."

"Who cares?" Gabi's fingers clutched her arms. "Either way, it's wrong. If mall security finds out, they'll throw us in jail. Or worse, call my mom."

Gabi's mom was pretty scary. The woman could dole out punishments like no one else.

"That's not going to happen," I said. "I have a plan."

"No offense, but that doesn't make me feel any better. Your schemes always backfire."

"Not all of them. And this one is simple." Well, the part I was letting Gabi in on, anyway. "Just get inside and snap a photo of us with Lance. Think about how crazed Courtney will be when she finds out we got to hang out with Lance and she didn't."

I could tell Gabi was holding back a smile at the mere thought of it.

"Come on," I said, egging her on. "I know you want to. Let's stick it to Courtney for a change. Make her jealous of us."

"I don't know, Angel. This sounds crazy."

I didn't want to hear any of her negativity. This was going to work. I knew what I was doing. "Are you in or not?"

"Well . . ." She hemmed and hawed.

"I'll take that as a yes," I said. She'd thank me later. *"Shh."* I held up my finger to my mouth as Gabi started to speak. "No backing out."

"Fine," she conceded. "I'll go meet Lance with you. But just how do you plan on getting past those guards?"

"Like this." With a wave of my arm, I made a trash can move ten feet forward. When one of the men went to go check it out, I made it move farther. Thank goodness I actually had one power mastered. It felt dangerous. It felt fun.

"What's going on?" the other guard asked.

"Some prank, I'm sure. I bet some kid is hiding in there," he said, chasing the can around the corner.

Now it was time to keep guard number two busy. With another simple movement, I made some guy's soda lurch forward. It splattered over the fake wall built to keep fans away from the side entrance. "Who did that?" the guard asked, walking toward the mob. I hoped I didn't get the guy in trouble, but I couldn't worry about it at that very moment.

It was now or never.

"Run," I said to Gabi.

We booked it to the door. I quickly opened it and pulled Gabi inside. She was about to have a date with destiny.

chapter

5

"Oh my gosh, oh my gosh, oh my gosh," Gabi whispered as we made our way through the store. "I can't believe we are really doing this. OH. MY. GOSH."

The last part was a shout. Because standing right in front of us was none other than Lance Gold himself.

And while he was hot on TV, he was a million—no, a zillion—times hotter in person. His hair was a brownish-red mess on top of his head—a perfect mess. Like it took days to make it look like that. His face had a light tan that highlighted his perfect features, and there was not a zit to be found. And his eyes. They were just like his name. Gold. Seriously. The color, the sparkle, everything. They were so mesmerizing that it was hard to take in much else. Like the fact that he was talking to us.

"Answer him," Gabi said, poking me in the side with her elbow.

"Huh?" I asked, snapping back to reality.

"I said, 'How'd you get in here?'" Lance questioned us. He didn't seem so thrilled to see us there, but I could tell he was trying to be nice. Which was exactly what I was counting on. If everything Gabi and the magazines said were true, then Lance would never be mean to a fan. He was a genuinely good guy. Maybe even good enough to go out with a girl who had just gotten her heart creamed by a jerk.

"Oh," I said. It was hard to talk and look at him at the same time. "We were invited. See, Gabi here, she was supposed to have a photo shoot with you. That's why you were originally scheduled to come to Pennsylvania in the first place. It got canceled. But the producer still gave us the okay to meet you." My storytelling ability under pressure was pretty awesome, if I do say so myself. I totally would have believed me.

"Nobody told me anything about it," he said.

"They probably just forgot." I flashed him a big smile, showing off my dimples. Everyone always said they made me look cute and sweet. I was hoping that translated into more believable as well.

"My manager never forgets anything," he answered.

"First time for everything." I was still smiling. However, the power of my dimples was not working. But if it came to it, I knew powers that would. "Anyway," I continued. "This is Gabi. Gabi, this is Lance Gold."

I nudged her forward.

"Hi," she said, putting out her hand. It was trembling. He took it, but he looked skeptical. Not like a guy falling in love. Or even one willing to go out on a mercy date.

"I really don't think you should be back here. You need to go before my manager sees you. She's not very fan friendly."

We couldn't go. He had to talk to Gabi and realize how cool she was. How she'd make the perfect girlfriend. "Sorry," Gabi said. "We don't want to bother you. We were just hoping to get a picture."

Yeah, and an engagement ring. Gabi was thinking too small. "I'll take it of the two of you," I offered. "Now get closer."

They just stood there.

"Lance, put your arm around Gabi."

He didn't do it. Instead he shook his head. "You

two really need to go before my manager sees you." His eyes darted to the door in the back of the store. There was an office back there.

Gabi walked back next to me and grabbed my arm. "Let's go, Angel."

I wasn't ready to give up. "Lance, wait! You didn't even get a chance to talk to Gabi. She's really funny. She'll have you laughing up a storm. Say something funny, Gabi."

"What are you doing?" she whispered at me, keeping a fake smile plastered on her face the whole time.

"Helping you," I whispered back. "And," I said, this time to Lance, "she's supersweet. I heard that you donate your time to charities. Well Gabi is always doing nice things. She never litters, once she saved a bird she found with a broken wing, and she even refuses to dissect frogs in science class."

"Nice," Lance said. But he didn't mean it. He was looking at the exit and his feet were all fidgety. I had to up my game.

"Know what else?" I asked him.

"Quit it, Angel," Gabi said, pinching me on the arm.

But I couldn't. My plan was going to work, I just needed to give it time. "Gabi would be perfect for you to take to all of your red carpet events. I read

36

the magazines, I know all those Hollywood stars are obnoxious. You don't need that. Not when there's someone as nice and as pretty as Gabi. She'd be the perfect date for you. Plus, she's been crushing on you forever!"

"Angel!" Gabi yelled.

"So what do you think?" I asked Lance, pretending I didn't hear Gabi's protest.

"Cut it out," Gabi answered for him. "I can't believe you're doing this to me again. Do you enjoy making a fool of me?" Gabi's hands were balled up into fists. She was squeezing them so hard, her knuckles were white.

"That's not what I'm doing. I'm helping you."

"Like how you helped with Marc? I told you to butt out of my love life."

"You guys really need to go," Lance said, glancing behind him. "My manager is going to hear you. It's going to get us all into trouble."

"We're so sorry," Gabi said, heading through the empty racks of clothes toward the door. "Let's go, Angel." Her voice was fierce.

"Just one date?" I asked Lance. "She's had a really bad day. This guy was a total jer—"

"Angel!" Gabi screamed again. And Lance just shook his head.

But I didn't care. I was not letting Gabi and Lance's romance die before it even started. I was going to go with my backup plan. I was going to cast a love spell on Lance and make him go nutty over Gabi. To see how incredible she really was. Then she'd forgive me. One kiss from Lance Gold and she'd totally forget that she'd ever been angry or hurt.

Yes, playing around with people's emotions was an advanced power. And my track record in that department was not exactly award-winning. But it was going to work. I was focused and wanted it more than anything. Two key ingredients to controlling my gift. Besides, it wasn't like I was trying to make the whole galaxy worship Gabi. I was just making *one* guy fall in love with *one* girl. It wasn't *that* big of a deal.

I put my arms out, directing them right at Lance. He needed to fall crazy in love. I directed all my power and concentration his way. "You're going to fall madly and passionately in love wi—"

"Angel," a woman who came rushing out of the back office yelled. How did she know my name?

But there wasn't time to think about it. Because she pushed Lance out of the way with one hand and she thrust the other one toward me. A wave seemed to rush through the air, going through me and Gabi, then rumbling through the stage curtain and hitting everyone in the vicinity.

My whole body felt warm, and then everything went black.

chapter

6

"Are you okay?" Gabi was standing over me. "Please tell me you're okay."

How did I end up on the floor? I slowly stood up.

"Say something! Angel!" Gabi cried.

"I'm fine." Only I was more than fine. I was fantastic. There was an almost electric energy spiraling through my body.

"What happened?" Lance asked.

"Nothing," his manager said. "Just stay away from her."

Stay away from her? Like I needed Lance Gold in my life? Who cared about him when there was someone clearly ten times more drool-worthy in the room?

"You didn't faint because I yelled at you, did you?" Gabi asked. "I'd never do anything to hurt you."

40

I guess she wasn't mad anymore. But it would have been hard to stay mad at me. I was incredibly charming. "I know," I told her.

She picked off some dust balls that stuck to my jeans. The cleaning staff really needed to do a better job on their floors. I was too special to walk around with dirt on me.

"Lance, I told you to go," his manager said.

What was her problem? How could she be more concerned with him when *I* was in the room?

"Don't worry," I told her. "He can stay. I'm leaving."

Lance wasn't that great. Not in comparison to yours truly—the most awesome person ever!

I didn't even want to be in the same space with someone who couldn't see that. So I brushed myself off and headed for the front entrance. People like me deserved way better than a side door. It was so out of the public eye, and I deserved bigger. I deserved to be the main event. So I walked right out through the curtain and onto the stage, my head held high.

A huge applause broke through the crowd. Naturally.

"I love you, Angel!" That was Max. His voice was definitely unmistakable.

"She's my true love!" Cole shouted back. "My girlfriend. My boo."

"Not for long," someone else said. "She's going to be mine."

I couldn't even make out what was said after that. There was too much screaming. Not that I could blame the crowd for fighting. If anyone was worth it, it was me.

A few people held up their phones and took pictures. I was definitely going to need copies.

"Angel, Angel, sign my shirt, pleaasseeee!" Courtney said, forcing a pen up toward me. Uck. Of course, she managed to get close. I couldn't be around someone like her. She was pathetic. I couldn't risk it rubbing off.

"Get away," I commanded.

"You heard her," someone else said, pushing Courtney away from the stage.

That gave me more breathing space, but it still wasn't enough. Other people immediately took her spot. And while they weren't as irritating as the mere sight of Courtney, they were still bothersome. There were screams, requests for pictures and autographs. It was too much. I couldn't think. My precious thoughts were getting away from me when they needed to be savored. I had to make an escape. Mere mortals couldn't appreciate someone like me. I was gifted, I could do special things. I was mind-blowingly cool.

I needed to go somewhere quiet where I could appreciate my magnificence in private. I needed to go home.

I jumped off the stage. Can you say huge mistake? People crowded around me as if one glance from me would make their lives complete. Which I guess was true. But still, it was too much. Strangers were tugging at my sleeves and trying to shake my hand. I understood it. It wasn't every day they got to be that close to greatness. But I wanted some "me time," too! I deserved it.

So with one hand motion, I parted the crowd, leaving a nice, empty path to the exit.

Perfect powers for a perfect girl.

And just like that, I left the mall.

chapter

7

"What are you doing out there?" my mom asked, her head poking out from the front door of our house.

"Just gazing." I had been standing there motionless for about twenty minutes.

"At what?"

"At me." I let out a long sigh and continued to look at my reflection in the window.

"Come inside," my mom said.

"I'm fine right here." I twisted my hair up into a bun. It looked hot. But maybe down was better. I let it fall loose again. Ahh, who was I kidding? My hair looked great whichever way I wore it.

"You know, we have actual mirrors inside."

She had a point. "Fine." I went in the house.

"I made a new potion for Auras-R-Us," she said.

"Try it for me." Aurasrus.com was a new-age website Mom ran. She sold all sorts of wacky, mystical products on it that she claimed could enhance your soul and aura. I had serious doubts.

"No, thanks."

"I need another opinion," she said. "I think I may have added too much lavender to this one. And you can't have a purifying potion with too much lavender. It just doesn't work."

She wasn't going to take no for an answer. So I decided to humor her. Then I could get back to my long to-do list and get some important things out of the way, like taking pictures of myself with my webcam.

I got comfy in the big Buddha chair in our kitchen. I bet I looked totally adorable sitting there with those pudgy Buddha arms engulfing me. I'd have to get a picture of that, too.

As soon as Mom placed a bowl of her concoction in front of me, I totally lost my appetite. I was overcome with a flood of warmth. There in the spoon was my reflection. And it was all distorted. I was like an abstract piece of art. So cool. I belonged in a museum.

"Well?" Mom asked.

How could I eat when my stomach was flopping all over the place? It was like what happened when Cole smiled at me, only even more intense. My heart sped up like it was the soundtrack to a really fast Mara's Daughters song. I couldn't get enough of myself. I moved the spoon around in front of me. Each twist gave me a new look. A new work of art. "Amazing."

"You didn't try it!" she shouted.

"What are you talking about?" I asked.

"You just called the potion amazing when you haven't even tasted it."

Sometimes moms could be so clueless. "I wasn't talking about your watered-down soup. I was talking about *me*. *I'm* amazing. Duh."

"Okay, what is going on here? What is wrong with you today?"

I couldn't hold back my laughter. "*Wrong* with *me*? Absolutely nothing. Anyone with eyes can see that."

The next thing I knew, Mom was placing six crystals in front of me. She must have been afraid Lou was going to pop in to try and get some face time with his fab daughter. Mom always brought out crystals when she got nervous about anything. It was fine with me. They were better than mirrors. I could see my reflection in them. Multiplied by ten. I was surrounded by dozens of Angels. Just like heaven.

"What did your father do to you?"

"Lou? Nothing. I'm not even speaking to him." I threw a kiss at the crystals. My reflections threw one back.

"This is definitely tied to the devil," Mom droned on. "You are not acting like you."

"Sorry," I said when I finally realized what was going on.

Mom was jealous. Jealous that I wasn't giving her any of my attention. It wasn't right. After all, the greatness that was me wouldn't even exist if it wasn't for her. So I tore my eyes away from the crystals. It was time to include Mom.

"What do you think?" I asked, showing her a full-lipped, pouty face like they did on that *Top Model* show. "Do you like this one?" Then I made another pout, this time only jutting out my bottom lip. "Or this one?"

Mom's eyes got superwide. She must have been awed that I was letting her help me decide which look to use. So much so that she couldn't even contain herself.

Out of nowhere, she did something I'd never seen her do before. She probably just wanted to share the moment with her partner in my creation.

And really, who could blame her?

"LOUUUUUUUUUUUU!"

chapter
✧ 8 ✧

A big burst of smoke appeared right next to me. It only clouded the air for a moment, but I was annoyed. That was a whole moment where I couldn't see myself. It was bad enough I had to waste time blinking and humoring my mother; I didn't need to lose more precious time dealing with an evil father.

Lou was standing to my right when the smoke evaporated. "What can I do for you, ladies?" he asked.

"You can start by undoing what you've already done," Mom told him.

"What are you talking about?" he asked.

Mom grabbed onto a crystal and squeezed it, which I found rude. That crystal was not a stress ball. It was a tool to reflect my beauty. "I am talking about your daughter. Just look at her."

Both of them trained their eyes on me. I knew Mom

wanted me to do my model faces for Lou to show him how gifted I was. But he didn't deserve it. A devil who went around teaching his minions to take good souls for the underworld shouldn't be rewarded. Even if that same devil claimed he wouldn't ever do it again.

But I didn't want to upset Mom. She didn't do anything wrong, and she had made the effort to get Lou there just to show me off. So I decided to do her a favor.

I made the best faces—better than just pouty. I threw in fierce, surprised, and happy. And you know what?

He didn't even appreciate it.

"I don't get it," he said. "What's going on?"

What was going on was that he didn't understand pure genius when he saw it. It was a miracle someone as great as me came from someone as awful as him.

I crossed my arms over my chest.

Hmmm. Why had I ever had issues with my boobs before? They seemed fine to me now. I pulled on the collar of my T-shirt and peered down inside. Yep. My chest was perfect just the way it was. And, it made sense my size was double-A. After all, you couldn't do any better than an A-plus!

"Angel?" my mom asked.

I took my head out of my shirt. "What?"

She just shook her head. Probably annoyed that I stopped paying attention to her. But it was hard when I had myself to think about. I was like the Eighth Wonder of the World.

I posed like an ancient Egyptian. Yeah, the pyramids had nothing on me. "Quick," I told Mom, "get the video camera. My beauty needs to be documented and sent to *National Geographic*. They're going to want to do a cover story on the world's newest gift to mankind."

Lou scrunched up his face. Maybe he was beginning to see how stupendous I was. About time.

"This is too much," Mom mumbled. "She can't get enough of herself." Well, obviously. "Angel," she said, "I just realized how well you can see yourself on the door to the oven."

She didn't need to tell me twice. I planted myself right in front of it. She was right. It beat the crystals—all of me, not just my face, was visible in the door.

"See," Mom told Lou.

It was sweet that she was trying to get him to realize how spectacular I was.

Lou moved toward me. I could see his legs in the stove door, and they were totally ruining the view.

I took a deep breath. I blocked him out. Instead, I focused on my eyes. My beautiful eyes.

I was soooo lovely. My heart was beating faster than before and my breath was shallow. I closed my eyes and leaned in closer to the stove.

A wave rushed through me. I opened my eyes and found myself KISSING the oven door. What was wrong with me? Who kissed their own reflection in a kitchen appliance?

I turned around. My parents were both staring at me.

"Feel better?" Lou asked.

No, I felt humiliated. I stood up and looked at him. "What did you do?"

"Took you out of the spell you were under," he said.

"Spell?!"

"Yep, from the looks of it, a love spell. And I think the real question here is what did *you* do?"

chapter

Love spell? On myself? Well, that would explain the mushy gushy feeling I had. But how did it happen? I was trying to make Lance fall in love with Gabi. Not *me* fall in love with *me*! This was truly embarrassing. I was being ridiculous. Not even Courtney spent that much time admiring herself. And she held the world's record in vanity.

"Well," Lou said. "Care to explain?" Both of my parents were still staring at me.

I couldn't. Lou knew that. My mom wasn't clued in to the fact that I had powers, and that's exactly how it needed to stay. When Lou first came into my life, she said it didn't matter if I inherited his special gift, that she'd love me no matter what. But when I lied and told her there was nothing magical about me, she seemed super-relieved. I knew she would be. Mom changed her name, her job, her whole life to get away from Lou and his evil ways. Having a daughter who took after him was not on her wish list.

"Beats me," I answered. "No clue how it happened." Ignorance was always effective. They couldn't blame me for something I knew nothing about.

Only Lou wasn't buying it. "Angel," he said in one of those I-know-you-know-more than-you're-letting-on voices.

"Maybe it was you," I accused him. "Did you do something to me?" I felt bad blaming Lou for a mess he had nothing to do with, but I was protecting my mother.

She moved between me and Lou. "What is going on? Was it you?" she asked him.

"No, and Angel knows that."

I chewed on two of my nails. What was I supposed to say? *Surprise, Mom! Not only do I have powers like my devil dad, but I've been using them to run a dating service and to stick it to my enemies?* I'd have been grounded until I turned twenty-two.

Their stares were getting uncomfortable.

"Well . . . ," my mom said.

"Fine, I'll tell you. But you can't get freaked out."

Mom sucked in some air and sat down at the table.

"See, well, it's, um, nothing." I paced around the

kitchen. "I just went to see Lance Gold at the mall, and I snuck backstage. I don't know what happened next. This woman, I guess it was his manager, came out of nowhere, and she knew my name, and the next thing I knew I was acting all weird." I blurted it all out really fast, minus a few unimportant details. Like me using my powers.

Mom shook her head. "That doesn't make sense."

"No, it doesn't," he said. "Harmony Gold wouldn't do that. Not unprovoked."

What? *Harmony Gold?* How did he even know who I was talking about? Maybe he knew her. Probably from the underworld. I decided to use that to my advantage. "You know, I actually thought she looked a little evil. Demonlike. And, well, we all know you can't trust a demon. Not even to follow your orders. Can't believe she messed with the devil's daughter, though. That was pretty gutsy."

"She's not a demon," Lou said. "She's an angel. A guardian angel."

chapter

✦ 10 ✦

A guardian angel! There were angels here on earth?! I don't know why I was so surprised. If there were demons running around the planet, why shouldn't there be angels, too?

"How do *you* know an angel?" I asked.

"A long time ago, I used to be one," he answered. "Until I decided to work for the other side."

I knew that. That was ancient history. "What I meant was how does she know what you're up to *now*? If it was so long ago, how does she know you have a thirteen-year-old daughter?"

"We still keep tabs on each other. And we have an understanding. I don't mess with the guardian angels, and they don't mess with me. Although I'm sure Harmony wasn't thrilled to get a visit from you."

"Maybe that's why she did the love spell," I said, using the info to enhance my lie. "She was afraid I was going to do something evil, and countered hate with love!"

Mom watched us, but seemed at a loss for words.

"I don't think—," he began.

"Why is she a manager then?" I asked, cutting him off. I didn't want the conversation to turn to me and my powers. It was better to keep Lou talking about angels. "And what does she want with Lance? If I were a real angel, I wouldn't waste my time working in the entertainment business. I'd join the Peace Corps or something."

"She's not just his manager. Harmony *Gold*. Lance *Gold*. She's his mother."

Whoa. "Lance is an angel, too? Then why is he on TV?"

"My guess? Because it would make the perfect cover for him to get to know the people he's supposed to help. Who wouldn't want a visit from their favorite star? In fact, he's not the only magical being in the arts." I knew that firsthand. I'd recently found out that Mara's Daughters was made up of demons. Though they seemed like good demons.

But I wouldn't bet my life—or soul—on that.

"Wait," Mom said, finally finding her voice. "Why would this woman, angel, whatever, put a love spell on Angel?"

"That's what I was saying, she was probably just protecting herself from Lou's evil spawn," I answered before Lou could.

"No." Lou shook his head. "She'd know better. I don't need a kid to do my bidding."

"I'm not a kid!"

He raised an eyebrow at me. Fine, maybe it wasn't the right point to argue even though I hated that they treated me like I was a child. But I had bigger issues at the moment. Like Mom's questions.

"Then why did she do it?" Mom pressed on.

"What did you do, Angel?" Lou asked.

I racked my brain for a good excuse. I must have had my very own guardian angel, because a second later the perfect answer came to me.

"I asked Lance for his autograph, and his mom probably thought I was trying to get him to sign over his soul, and so she cast a spell on me."

Mom nodded. She bought it. Yes! Close call averted.

"I'm going to go take a nap now." I wanted to get

away before they asked any more questions.

"Not so fast." Lou stopped me. "Time to fess up, Angel."

"Fess up to what?" Mom asked.

"Are you going to tell your mother or am I?" Lou asked.

"Tell me what?" Mom stood up.

I didn't say a word. I couldn't.

"Angel has pow—"

"No," I screamed. "Don't listen to him."

Mom threw her hands up over her ears and started to bang them as if they were bongo drums. "I can't hear anything," she said in a really loud voice. "What's happening?"

What had I done? Oh no. I knew what was happening. I needed to calm down. To get my emotions in check. To stop my powers from going off on their own.

But I couldn't.

This was huge.

My mother couldn't find out my secret.

Mom looked panicked. She moved to the corner of the room where her giant totem pole was resting. She thought it kept evil at bay. Obviously it didn't since the devil was still right there.

"Stop!" I cried.

And she did. Mom stopped, frozen. Because she *was* frozen. I'd turned my very own mother into a statue.

chapter

11

"Ohmygoshohmygoshohmygosh," I said over and over again as I shook my mom. But she didn't budge. "Don't worry, I'll fix you. You won't be frozen forever. I promise." I knew she couldn't hear me, but still . . .

"I got it," Lou said.

As he started to wave his hand in front of her face, I yelled, "Wait."

Talk about horrible. I was stopping the devil from fixing my mom. Did that make me worse than him?

"You don't want me to undo this?" he asked, his eyes lasering into mine.

"Of course I do. Just not yet. We need to talk first." Really, it was for Mom's own good. I needed to convince Lou not to tell her about my special gift so she'd go on thinking I was the same sweet, powerless girl she loved. Not some evil, Mom-freezing, spell-casting monster.

"Waiting a few minutes won't hurt her, will it?"

When Lou told me there wouldn't be any lasting side effects, I made him move with me to the living room. I couldn't have the conversation I was about to have in front of my mother—statue or not. It weirded me out.

"I'm listening." Lou made himself comfortable on the couch, like he was at home.

I didn't like it, but kept silent about it. One battle at a time. I stood, arms crossed, a few feet away. "You promised you wouldn't tell Mom about my powers."

"That's not what I said."

"Oh, right, another one of your loopholes to get out of a deal. *You're* not going to tell Mom. You're going to make *me* do it. I should have known not to trust the devil."

Lou crossed his hands in his lap. "There's no loophole. If you remember correctly, I told you next time you tried advanced powers without permission, I was going to tell your mother everything. And last time I checked, trying to make someone fall in love with you is an advanced power."

"I wasn't trying to make anyone fall in love with me." That was true. I was trying to make Lance fall in love with Gabi.

"Don't you think it's time to stop lying?" he asked.

"Ha!" I said so loudly it could have jarred Mom from her statue state. "That's hilarious coming from *you*. The guy who has done nothing but lie to me from the minute he came into my life."

"I haven't lied to you." Lou stood up and stepped toward me.

I backed up. "Um, how about telling me you'd never take a good soul for the underworld, and then I catch you teaching one of your underlings how to do it, which is virtually the same thing?"

"Angel, I've explained this. I didn't know what he was up to. He only came to me when everything got out of control. I was only helping him fix the mess he created. Powers can cause major problems when you haven't been trained thoroughly. I think you may know something about that. But I've changed. The guy who collected good souls was the old me. The new one only guards the underworld, keeping evil souls from escaping."

"Don't believe you."

"I know," he said. "And I want to fix that. Prove to you I can be the kind of father you can count on."

"Not telling Mom about my powers would be a good start."

Lou shook his head. "Don't you think this family has had enough secrets?"

I plopped down in the chair. "One more wouldn't hurt."

"Angel." Lou sat on the arm of the couch.

Telling Mom was too risky. It would just give her more to worry about, if that was even possible. I balled myself up in the chair.

"Why don't you start by telling me what really happened at the mall?"

"It was nothing. I was trying to make Lance fall for Gabi, and his mom came out in the middle of the spell. She said my name and threw one of her hands in my direction. And that's all I remember."

Lou nodded. "She put up a shield. It sent the power you were sending out back to you."

"But then wouldn't I have fallen in love with Gabi, not myself?"

"Hmmm," he said, his hand stroking his chin. "Tell me exactly what happened, and don't leave anything out."

I went over the whole story with him again.

"Ahh, that's it," Lou said, cutting me off in the middle. "Harmony called out your name in the middle of it. Your thoughts must have switched from Gabi to yourself."

"But how did she even know what I was up to? That I was even using my powers?"

"It's her job," he said.

"Right," I mumbled. "Because she's a guardian angel."

"Because she's a *mother*. And she thought her child was in danger."

I knew where this was headed . . .

"And a mother should know what her child is up to. Especially when her child is in over her head." This was clearly no longer about Lance.

"Good thing *I* know what *I'm* doing," I told him. "I'm safe and sound. There's no need to worry Mom."

"She wants to know what's going on with you."

I looked away from Lou. "And she does. She's just missing a few details."

"Important ones."

"Not to me." Me not telling her about my powers was no different than me not telling her that I snuck into horror movies when she thought I was at some Disney film, or Gabi not telling her mom she stuffed her face with junk food whenever given the opportunity. Moms didn't need to know every little detail.

"Trust me," he said, "the fact that you have powers will matter to your mother. And you know that."

Yes. I did know that. Which was precisely the reason I didn't want to tell her anything.

Not that what I wanted factored into any of this. Before I knew it, Lou snapped his fingers. We were back in the kitchen.

"It's time, Angel."

chapter

✧ 12 ✧

"What happened?" Mom asked when Lou put her back to normal. She squeezed the giant totem pole. "Will somebody please tell me what is going on here?"

I shrugged my shoulders. "Beats me."

Yeah, I know. Lou had just given me that after-school-special speech—the one that was supposed to motivate me to come clean and confess everything. But this wasn't TV, where the truth would result in a big group hug and ice cream sundaes. This was real life, where the truth would result in karma-cleansing baths and exorcisms before bedtime just to make sure my head didn't spin three hundred sixty degrees like those girls in the horror movies.

"Your daughter is what happened," Lou said. "She has my powers."

Traitor.

Mom looked like she was going to pass out. She clutched the big wooden stick for support. "For how long?"

"A while now," he said.

He was totally selling me out. "Don't believe him, Mom. He's still evil. I even heard him trying to take a good soul."

Lou lowered his head and his voice. "I know you're mad that I'm telling your mother the truth, but she deserves to know." He looked back up at me. "I even understand you making up lies about me. You're angry. I hope you'll be able to forgive me."

No way! He was turning this around on me. Making me look like the bad guy. "Mom, he did take that soul, I swear."

Lou shook his head slightly and put this sad look on his face. What a faker!

Mom looked at both of us. Then her eyes rested on me—and they were filled with anger.

"You don't believe him, do you?" I cried out. "Over your own daughter? He's the devil! He majored in lying."

"And it seems you're taking right after him."

"I am NOT lying. He took a soul. That's what he does." She was taking his side over mine. Unbelievable.

"Fine," Mom said, her nails tearing into the wood of the totem pole. "Then why don't you tell me what happened today."

I couldn't. Not with her looking at me like that.

"Lou?" she asked.

"Last chance, Angel," he warned me.

I folded my arms and kept my mouth shut.

No one said anything for what felt like days. Lou finally broke the silence. "I'm sorry, Angel," he said. Then he told Mom everything. And not just what I did today with the love spell. Everything. All those mess-ups I've had with my powers since Lou entered my life. He filled her in on everything. Nothing was left out. NOTHING!

And Mom just stood there quietly taking it all in.

My insides felt like goo, but I couldn't move. I felt like a prisoner listening to all the charges being read against me in court. Lou was the prosecution. And Mom was the judge. And from the expression on her face, a pretty unforgiving one.

"Do you have anything to say?" Mom asked me when Lou finally finished.

"Not guilty?" I said with a small smile.

Mom did not find it humorous. Not at all.

"Angel Kindness Garrett!" she shouted.

This was serious. Mom was using my middle name. "What?" I asked. "It's not my fault I have powers." I looked right at her. "Besides, didn't you say you'd love me no matter what? I guess that was a lie."

"You know I love you. And I'm not mad that you have powers. You can't help that. I'm mad that you lied about it. And I'm mad that you went around recklessly using them."

"I wasn't reckless," I objected.

"You tried to cast a love spell," Lou offered. "That's reckless."

Why didn't he butt out of it? This was between my mom and me. "I was trying to help a friend."

"You were playing with people's emotions," Mom said.

"People do that all the time!" It was true. People messed around with feelings every day. I'd lost count of the number of times Courtney made Gabi or me feel like a turd. "I was just trying to help Gabi feel better!"

"That doesn't matter," Mom said.

"Doesn't matter? People were messing with my best friend. Saying all sorts of nasty things. I had to do something."

Mom raised her hand to stop me. "I don't want

to hear the excuses, Angel. You're grounded." She slammed the totem pole on the ground, finalizing her decision.

Lou nodded in agreement.

"That's not fair!" I screamed. I was fuming. "You don't get it. If you guys were younger, then you'd understand. Then you'd see."

A swirl of red smoke snaked around my parents. I watched as the little lines on their foreheads and around their eyes vanished, their faces got fuller, jawlines softer, and the little patches of gray in their hair disappeared.

Lou shrunk an inch and Mom's stance changed. Their skin seemed tighter.

They were morphing before my very eyes.

Morphing into their younger selves.

My parents had become teenagers.

chapter

13

"Mom?" I asked cautiously, eyeing her.

"*Mom?*" she elongated the word in the way you might if it were the most insulting word you could possibly call someone. Her voice was an octave higher than normal. "Are you talking to *me*?"

I should have kept my mouth shut! I knew I was angry. When was I finally going to learn that when I'm emotional, I need to be extra careful about what I say or my powers go off?

"Don't panic," I told Mom and tried to take my own advice. "I'll make you look your age again." I shrugged my shoulder at her. "But you look pretty awesome this way." She really did. I had never seen pictures of young Mom. She kept her past pretty secret. But she was gorgeous. Why couldn't I have taken after her?

Mom backed up against the door. "What are you

talking about?! WHAT IS GOING ON HERE? *Where am I*?"

Oh wait—this wasn't right. Mom didn't just *look* like a teen. She thought she *was* one. And now she was freaking out. It was worse than I'd thought. "It's okay," I said in my most soothing voice possible.

I definitely wasn't helping Mom relax. She was visibly shaking and her breath was short and fast. I handed her a paper bag to breathe into. But she just swatted my hand away. "I want to go home," she said. "How did I get here?"

What was I supposed to say to that? That the devil made me do it? Teen Mom didn't even know he was real, let alone that she'd married him and had his child.

OH. MY. GOD.

The devil. I forgot about him.

If Mom thought she was her teen self, then so did Lou. And who knew what that meant? He used to be an angel. Hopefully I sent him back to that point in his life. "Lou?" I asked.

"Yes," he answered. He was studying me, the room—taking everything in. He looked way too suspicious to be an angel. But his eyes kept circling back to my mother. I wasn't sure if it was because in

73

her current state she looked like easy soul-stealing prey or because he thought she was hot. But from the way the corners of his mouth were turned up into a small smile, I guessed it was the latter.

"Do you know who I am?" I asked.

"I have some ideas."

What did that mean?

"Well, I don't," Mom whispered. The color was gone from her face. "I gotta get out of here." She opened the back door, but with a wave of my hand, I pushed it shut.

Mom screamed. She tried the door again, yanking at the doorknob. I had no choice but to make sure she couldn't get out. But she wasn't giving up. She grabbed a crystal and threw it through the door's window, shattering the glass.

She was determined to leave. But I couldn't let her. With another hand motion I moved her to the other side of the kitchen.

That caused her to scream again. A long, shrieky one. But it did make her stop trying to escape. Instead, she sank to the floor and started to cry.

"I'm sorry, I'm sorry," I said and raced to her. "It's going to be okay. I just can't let you go. Not the way you are right now."

But she didn't want to hear it. Not from me. She covered her head with her hands and began to rock. "Please don't hurt me, please don't hurt me," she kept saying over and over.

"*Hurt you*? I'd never hurt you. You're my mom."

"Why do you keep saying that?" she asked.

I looked to Lou. I was hoping he'd say something that would help the situation. Anything! But he just stood there waiting for me to answer. He wanted to hear as much as she did.

There was nothing to say, nothing that would make sense to her, so I kept silent, and her sobs got louder.

"Help me," I said to Lou.

"Why should I?" he asked. Ugh. Teens could be so frustrating.

"For her," I said, pointing to Mom, and prayed my hunch was right. That Lou was completely taken by her looks. "Do you want her to be like this? All afraid of powers and magic? How will you win her over then? Wouldn't it be easier to get her to like you if she just accepted it all?"

"She'd like me either way," he said, all full of himself. "I'm pretty charming."

Teen devil was even more annoying than the adult version. "Look at her," I said.

75

"I am," he said, his smile getting bigger.

I rolled my eyes. "I *mean*, see how upset she is?" Mom was balled up on the floor. "If you like her, don't you want her to be happy? Not some crying mess?"

Lou pursed his lips together. Then he finally spoke. "Fine," he said. "But for her, not for you. *We're* not done."

My parents didn't know each other as teens. They met at NYU. But it seemed no matter what age Lou was, he felt a connection with Mom.

Lou waved his hand in front of my mother and a moment later she was on her feet. "Okay . . . ," she said impatiently, her hands on her hips. "What am I doing here?"

This time there were no tears. There was no hyperventilating, no trying to escape. There was just major attitude.

"Well," I said, "umm, my mother asked you here to . . . to babysit me."

"Yuck," she whined. "I hate babysitting."

And while she wasn't happy about the circumstances, she didn't question them. Lou did it! He made her go with the flow!

Mom crinkled her nose at me. "Aren't you a little old to have a babysitter?" she asked.

"My mom is super-overprotective." Understatement of the year. "It's not my fault you're here."

"My guess is that this is very much your fault," Lou said.

Did he remember?

Suddenly, Mom seemed to notice Lou for the first time. As she looked him over, her eyes got wide. "Hi," she said and batted her eyelashes. "I'm Maggie." Maggie was the name she went by as a kid—before she changed it.

"Lou," he said and flashed her a dimpled smile.

Mom cocked her head to the side and bit her lip.

No way!! They were flirting with each other!

"So what were you saying about this being her fault?" Mom asked, not taking her eyes off of him for an instant.

"Some magical beings need more supervision than others," he said, leaving out the part that he was the devil and needed a chaperone more than anyone.

"Totally," Mom said, like she knew what Lou was talking about.

But I guess she did. At least part of it—like powers. I *had* asked Lou to make her accept everything.

"So, Lou," she said, flipping her hair over her shoulder. "A guy like you, I bet you're super-powerful."

He just winked at her.

"Come on," she said and swatted his arm, letting her hand linger there. "You're not going to tell me what you can do?"

"You really want to know?" he asked.

"What do you think?" she responded, her voice practically giddy.

I could not believe what I was seeing. My mom was a monster flirt. And she was hitting on the devil!

"I bet you can make Harry Potter look like a store magician compared to you," Mom gushed on.

Wait a second. "You know who Harry Potter is?"

Mom rolled her eyes at me, and then made the "cuckoo" gesture with her hand. "Who doesn't?"

Oohhhhhhh. So I had turned my parents into *modern-day* teens. They had their old personalities complete with up-to-date useless knowledge. Too bad they couldn't remember me or their actual, adult lives.

"I can do all sorts of stuff," Lou told her.

"Like what?" Mom asked.

"Like anything your heart desires. Just name it."

Talk about cheese! But Mom was eating it up.

"Anything?" she asked.

"Anything," he answered.

Mom giggled. Giggled! She should have been freaking out. She was dealing with the devil!

"Then how'd you get stuck here babysitting with me?" she asked, flipping her hair again.

"Couldn't leave you alone with her." He pointed at me. "I wouldn't want something to happen to you. She could be dangerous."

Me?! What about him? If Lou wasn't going to reveal his true identity to Mom, then I was going to do it for him.

"Do you realize he's the devil?" I yelled. I expected Mom to have another breakdown, to sink to the floor in a frenzied panic. But she didn't. She just twirled a strand of hair around her finger and said, "Oooh, bad boys are always more fun."

"You *are* kidding me, right?" I demanded. "We're not talking about some guy who just skips school or stays out after his curfew. We're talking about the Prince of Darkness."

"Even better," she said and winked at Lou. "I've always wanted to date a prince."

This was too much. "He's evil!"

"He's probably just misunderstood," Mom countered and rolled her eyes at me.

I opened my mouth to object, but Lou cut me off.

He was totally eating up everything Mom had to say and loving every second of it.

"Maggie, can you give us a few minutes?" he asked her. "I want to talk to this girl. See what she's up to. Make sure you're safe around her."

Safe? From *me*? I had a lot to say to that, but I didn't. Mom nodded. Her eyes were sparkling. She was totally smitten by Lou and his knight-in-shining-armor act. "Okay, I'll go see if there's anything decent to wear in this house. I have no idea why I'm in these mommy jeans. Gross."

Clearly, she didn't remember that this was her house. How could she just go rummaging through other people's stuff? "Uh, hello?" I said. "You can't go through the closets."

"Why not?"

"They're not yours."

"So?" she asked, like I was the one who said something stupid.

This was nuts. I couldn't believe I was having this conversation with her. Not that I got to finish it. Mom ran out of the room, sneaking a look back at Lou, before I could say anything else.

"So let me guess," Lou said the moment she was out of earshot. "You're just another angel trying to get me to reclaim my wings and come home? I already told the last guy and now I'm telling you. I'm done. I'm sick of being an angel. I'm never going back. It's time for me to shine."

This was bad. Way bad. Lou was back at the point in his life where he decided to go out on his own. Where he decided to become the devil.

"That's not it," I said, holding up my fingers in the Girl Scout pledge. I told him everything. How he was my father, how I inherited his powers, how I accidentally turned him back to his teen self. Everything.

But he didn't buy it. His eyes turned into little slits. "You might have been able to summon me here. But no way you'd be able to do something that big. Not if I were as powerful as you said. Not some little girl. Not to me."

"Only I did. I'm your daughter. Your powers *are* my powers."

"I don't have a daughter."

"You will."

He shook his head. His hands were tightening into fists and little energy waves were emanating from them. They formed a ball made of light and electricity. He was getting angry. At me! And who knew what this

Lou was capable of. "What's your game? Who put you up to this?" he asked.

"No one. Just calm down." I needed to say something he'd buy. I was actually getting scared of him. Was he going to throw that energy ball at me? At his own kid? What would that do? Transport me to another galaxy? Or worse? "I made it all up," I said.

"Why?" he asked.

"Because that's what, um, little sisters do, right?"

"I don't have a sister, either."

The energy waves were getting bigger.

"Wait," I said, trying to weave together a believable story as fast as I could. "You don't have a sister that you *know* of. But you do *have* one. I'm your half sister, Angel. I grew up on earth and just found out about you and my powers. I called you here to meet you. Honest. Look at the resemblance." I smiled, showing off the dimples. "And my eyes. See. I just wanted to meet you."

The energy waves went away. Lou was buying it.

"Trust me. You don't want to be a part of my family. I'm waging war with some powerful people. And I don't need some kid getting in the way. Do not summon me again. Got it?" He looked like he meant it. This Lou was not to be messed with.

"Hey," Mom said, skipping back into the room.

Lou's whole demeanor changed. He went from standing rigid and ready to attack me to Mr. Relaxed. He gave her a huge smile. He was totally crushing on her. Big time.

"Go back to your normal age, go back to your normal age," I said over and over again. But it wasn't happening. Mom just kept going on and on about her clothes.

"I was able to find this top in the back of a closet," Mom said inspecting her shirt. It was the one-sleeve black tee I had created with my powers ages ago. Mom had confiscated it and said no daughter of hers would ever go out of the house in it—that it was too risqué. Apparently teen Mom didn't think there was a problem with it. "But I couldn't find any decent jeans."

Please return to your normal ages! I thought, trying to wake my powers up, to force them to undo what I had just done. Focusing had worked for me in the past, but it wasn't doing anything for me now. I tried waving my hands the way Lou had to make Mom all accepting, closing my eyes and wishing, and I even made up a little poem/spell and said it a dozen times: "It's time to get everything on track, to your real ages you must go back. Okay, Mom and Lou, it's back

83

to adulthood for the two of you. So please this time, powers abide by my rhyme."

My poem didn't work. My parents weren't aging. They were still teens. I couldn't reverse what I had done.

"I could help you find a new outfit," Lou said, ignoring me and taking Mom's hand. "The world and beyond is at your disposal."

And Mom was smiling. It didn't bother her that Lou was going to use his devil powers for her. She actually liked it. This was definitely not the Mom I knew.

"Wait. You can't go. What about me?"

"I think you'll be just fine on your own," Lou said.

And with a wave of his hand, my parents were gone.

chapter

✦ 14 ✦

I'd just set the devil—the old, well, actually, young incarnation of him, anyway—loose on the world. To do who knows what?!

Lou had finally sworn off taking souls. And what did I do? Sent him back to his old tricks. With my mother as his sidekick. This was seriously wrong.

Where could they have gone? Lou said the world or beyond was at my mom's disposal. What would teen Mom pick? Probably somewhere with a lot of guys so she could toss her hair some more.

I leaned against the wall, banging my head back a couple of times. How could I have been so careless? How could I have let them leave as their young selves? I was at a loss.

My mom's attitude was bad enough. But Lou's was bound to be worse. Having a young devil on the loose put the whole world (as in universe!) in jeopardy. Who knew how many souls he'd try to take? I needed to stop him. To track him down. But how?

Summoning him was out of the question. Not that I knew how to go about it, anyway. But even if I did, he'd probably pulverize me with an energy ball for taking him away from his busy evil deeds and my mom. I needed to go to him. To find him and talk some sense into him. Yeah, because that would totally work. I'm sure the devil loved to be lectured by a thirteen-year-old.

But I couldn't worry about that now. First I had to find him. Then I could deal with how to get through to him.

Okay, how to reach him? His hPhone! The hPhone was like an iPhone, only with otherworldly applications. Lou probably had it with him. I could just call him.

I grabbed my cell. *One hundred twelve missed calls! What? Who could want to reach me that badly?*

Please let it be Mom and Lou coming to their senses.

As I reached to dial, the phone vibrated. I didn't recognize the number. "Hello?" I answered.

"Finally, I've been trying you forever."

"Max? Is that you?"

"Yep. Turn on channel five. I have a surprise for you."

A surprise? Surprises never ended well. I raced to the living room, turned on the TV, and braced for the worst. And that's pretty much what I got.

The news was on. Some blond reporter guy was doing a live broadcast from the mall about the Lance signing. There was Max standing behind him, blowing a kiss!

"That's for you, Angel," he said into the phone.

"You're on the phone with Angel?" someone off-camera asked.

Cole's head popped on-screen. The reporter tried to shoo him away. "I miss you, Angel. I love you. Where are you?"

What was happening? Why were they acting like this?

All of a sudden, a bunch of other people chimed in. They were waving at the camera, sending me their love.

Then I remembered.

They were all smitten with me. When I'd left the mall they had practically bombarded me with compliments and flattery. I hadn't paid much attention, but they were definitely crazed.

Lance's mother hadn't just sent the love spell back at me. It went way beyond that. Everyone standing in the vicinity of the stage was affected! Max, Cole, Gabi, Courtney—gobs of people were now infatuated with me. I had my very own fan club. And no idea how to fix it.

I dropped down onto the couch and just stared at the TV.

What came on-screen next was even more disturbing than my love-struck posse. It was Lou. And my mom.

She sidled herself up next to the reporter and winked at him.

Lou watched her lick her lips at the guy. Then with a wave of his arm, he pushed the crowd, including the reporter, to the side.

Mom laughed and put her arms around Lou. Had she been trying to make him jealous? If so, it was working! He put his arms around her and held her tight. They just stood there for a moment looking at each other. Then Lou planted a huge kiss right on Mom's lips for every channel five watcher, including me, to see.

Gross! If Lou ever got back to normal, I was going to make him erase that memory from my brain. Because watching your parents, even younger versions of them, make out was incredibly puke-inducing.

I had to turn away, only looking back at the screen when I heard Lou speak. "It's my show now," he said, pulling a grinning Mom closer toward him. If that was even possible!

Then he snapped his finger. And just like that, the TV went black. I reached for the remote. The other channels worked. But the live report from the mall was gone.

"Max!" I screamed into the phone. "What's going on? What's happening there?"

But there was no answer. The line was dead. I tried calling him back. Nothing. The same went for Cole and Gabi.

There was no communication coming from the mall.

Which could only mean one thing.

The devil was up to something.

chapter

My calves were on fire, I was biking so hard. I had to get back to the mall. I couldn't believe I was making a second trip there in one day. I don't even like shopping. But this wasn't about shopping. This was about stopping Lou from being Lou.

And that definitely warranted a return visit to the mall.

Who knew what I'd find when I got there? The whole place was probably a mini-underworld. I didn't really know what the underworld looked like, but I always pictured lots of flames and people shoveling coal. My classmates were probably chained together, forced to do whatever the devil said.

And my mom?! What was with her? I wanted to blame Lou—say it was his powers making her act this way. Only I had a feeling that wasn't the case. Lou made her accept her circumstances, but he didn't turn her into a flirt or a troublemaker. That was all her. What happened to the goody-two-shoes woman who punished me for every little thing? Like even sticking my tongue out when I was five? This Mom wore sexy clothes, engaged in PDA, and dated a bad boy. How dare she be so hard on me all these years when I'm way better behaved than she ever was? She had some serious explaining to do.

To get my mind off my parents, I checked my voice mail. The inbox was full. There were messages from Max, Cole, Gabi—everyone who had my cell phone number. Even Courtney, Lana, and Jaydin, who all had it from the three seconds we were friends.

They all thought I was incredible. And I'll be honest, the first few messages were fun to hear. Cole gushing about how he was the luckiest guy ever to get to have me for a girlfriend. How he needed me to come back to the mall for him. And how I was beautiful, smart, funny, breathtaking, inspiring, etc. Basically every nice adjective he could think of before the phone cut him off. But that didn't stop him. He called back and listed a slew more until the message reached the time limit again. I thought I'd never get tired of hearing him say cool things about me. But after a couple of minutes . . . I got bored. He was just saying the same stuff over and over again. The same with everyone else.

There were about three more messages by the time I pulled up to the mall. I didn't bother listening. There was no need. Because unless I could figure out a way to reverse what Lance's mom had done, I was about to hear all the compliments live and in person.

My public was waiting inside just a few feet away.

This was going to be a total mess.

chapter
✦ 16 ✦

I put the hood of my sweatshirt over my head and pulled the strings tight, making sure to keep my face toward the floor. It'd be a lot easier to deal with this without a group of people following me around.

With a deep breath, I pushed open the door to the mall. I wasn't greeted by flames or a demon army. It was just the mall. Busier than usual. But still, just the mall. I wasn't relieved, though. On television, the devil had said it was his show. Lou had to be up to something. The question was what.

Trying to avoid people was harder than I thought it would be. Staring at my feet made it impossible to see where I was going. Or what was going on around me. I needed help. I needed Gabi.

I made my way to the security desk and begged

the guard to page her. A few minutes later, Gabi rounded the corner.

"Ang—," she screamed.

"*Shhh,*" I warned her and grabbed her arm, pulling her into the Juicy Couture store. I pulled a dress off the rack and went back to the dressing rooms. Gabi followed.

"That's going to look amazing on you. But everything does," she gushed.

"Knock it off," I told her. I hadn't brought her back there to get compliments. I brought her back there to try and undo the spell so that she could help me with my other problem. My Lou problem. "You've been infected by my powers. They're what's making you think I'm a superstar."

"You are," Gabi said.

"Gabi, listen to me. You need to snap out of this. Think about it. Isn't it much more likely that you're under a spell, and I'm still the same regular girl I was this morning? The same girl you were furious at for messing with your love life. Come on, you have to know I'm not some idol?"

I could almost see her processing what I said.

"Nope. You're Angel Garrett, the most fabulous, incredible, wonderful person ever. And trying to convince Marc and Lance to go out with me was sweet. You knew how much I liked them, and you went out of your way to help me. I'm sorry I got angry. That was wrong. I should have appreciated what you were trying to do." Hopefully she'd remember that statement when I reversed the spell. "You're the best friend ever," she went on. "How lucky am I?"

Lucky? Not very.

"Now just relax," I told her. "I'm going to use my powers on you. Let's keep our fingers crossed that it works out better this time."

"Cool!" she said, opening up her arms, ready to embrace the power. "Bring it on."

Obviously, she wasn't thinking straight. There were no questions, no lectures, no warnings about what could go wrong, no trying to come up with an alternate solution. She was just happy to help.

Put Gabi back to normal. Put Gabi back to normal. I thought it, I said it, I focused on it as hard as I could.

"Well?" I asked her. "Do you still love me?"

"Of course I do! You're my best friend."

"Yeah, but sometimes you get annoyed with me, right?"

Gabi shook her head back and forth violently. "I

95

don't understand how I ever could have been mad at you. You're too wonderful. I'll try to be worthy of you. I promise. You'll see. I'll be the best best friend ever. Someone who deserves to hang out with you."

Why weren't my powers working?

"Are you girls all right in there?" the saleslady asked.

"*Are* we?" Gabi asked me. "You're not mad at me, are you? I hope not."

I rolled my eyes at her. "We're fine," I yelled to the woman. Only we weren't. Not as long as Gabi was under my spell.

"Thank goodness," Gabi said. "I don't think I could live knowing you were upset with me."

That was going too far. "Listen to me," I said to Gabi, holding up my hands. I stopped myself before I grabbed her and shook her. "I'm not all that. Okay? I'm not even such a great friend a lot of the time. Got it?"

Gabi blinked a few times. Then she crossed her arms around her stomach. "No kidding, you aren't. Ughh. What am I doing in here with you?"

"What?" I asked.

"I said, 'Why would I want to go shopping with someone disgusting like you?'"

Oh no! I hadn't undone the spell. I'd reversed it!

Instead of having Gabi love me, I made her hate me.

"Gabi, you don't really think I'm disgusting. I'm your best friend. We've been best friends since nursery school. What you're feeling isn't real. We're friends. I can fix this." I held onto her shoulders. "You like me. You don't hate me. You—"

"Help!" Gabi screamed and pushed me aside. She ran right out of the dressing room.

"What's wrong?" the saleslady asked, rushing over.

"Her," Gabi said, pointing at me. "She's what's wrong. Don't let her anywhere near me. She's the devil."

chapter
✦ 17 ✦

"Ha-ha!" I said, shooting Gabi a how-could-you-do-that-to-me look. "She's joking. I'm not the devil."

"Just his daughter," Gabi put in. Then she ducked down behind a display of shoes. "Watch it," she warned the saleswoman. "She'll probably try to make you her own personal shopper servant."

The saleswoman rubbed her temples.

"I'm not the devil or his daughter," I told her.

"No kidding," she said.

Oh right . . . I forgot that normal people wouldn't believe that the actual devil would be hanging out at the mall.

"Now if you'd both please leave the store. This isn't a playground," the woman continued.

"You're kicking me out for trying to help you?" Gabi asked, peering up at her. "Fine. Don't blame me when you're cursed."

Gabi gave me one last look and then she made a break for it.

I had no choice. I chased after her.

"Wait up," I yelled. It was a good thing she was a horrible runner. I was able to catch right up.

"I'll scream," she warned, "if you come any closer."

"Fine," I said. "I don't want to hurt you. I just want everything back to normal."

"This *is* normal," she said.

"No, it's not. We're friends, remember? Do you even know why you hate me?" I wanted to move toward her. But I was afraid she'd make a scene. So I stayed put.

Gabi ticked off reasons on her fingers. "You use your powers on me, you're dangerous, you ditched me for Courtney a couple of months ago, you're selfish, and you totally humiliated me in front of Marc and Lance Gold."

It might have been the spell talking, but that didn't mean it wasn't true. Gabi was right. I had been awful. I owed her. I was going to see that she was happy if it was the last thing I ever did. "I'd never hurt you. Not on purpose. Never."

"Well, you did."

"I'm sorry. It won't happen again," I promised. And it wouldn't. I was going to make everything up to her. Starting with Lance.

"Why should I believe you?"

"Because we're best friends."

She snorted. "Not really."

"Then because you know my secret. I can't risk you telling anyone else. Promise not to, and I'll leave you alone."

Gabi bit her lip.

"Please," I said.

"Okay. But I'm only doing it so I don't have to deal with you ever again."

"You don't really mean that."

I didn't even realize that I took a step forward until Gabi screamed my name.

"Angel Garrett, you're already breaking your promise."

"I'm not, I'm sorry. It was an accident." I backed up. "See, I'm moving away."

But there wasn't really anywhere for me to go. Because Gabi's scream had attracted a crowd. A whole bunch of people were headed our way.

"Did you say Angel?" someone I didn't even recognize asked.

100

"Yes!" another cheered. "I love her."

"Move," Courtney elbowed them. "Don't you see I'm trying to get through?"

"Get away while you can," Gabi said.

"What's your problem?" Courtney sneered. "Well, other than the obvious ones like that you're a complete loser. But I would have thought you'd be jumping up and down to see Angel." Courtney may have had newfound feelings for me, but the ones she had for Gabi were the same as always. Pure contempt.

"Not quite," Gabi said. "She's just like *you*. Evil."

"You think I'm like Angel?" Courtney asked, standing even straighter. "I guess even losers know greatness when they see it."

"Please," Gabi said. "She's not great. She's awful." She turned to Cole. "You were right to dump her before."

Sometimes I truly hated my powers.

"She's not awful," Cole said, squeezing his way through the fan club that formed around me. "She's Angel. She's . . ." He didn't finish. Instead he just leaned in and kissed me. In front of everyone.

"Not fair," Reid said. "I want to kiss her." The same Reid who was dating Lana Perkins.

Crazy.

I pulled away from him. Don't get me wrong. I liked when he kissed me. And when he stuck up for me. Only this time it didn't feel like I was kissing Cole. More like a pod person. Like I was in one of those body-snatcher movies. Where someone looked like Cole and sounded like Cole, but wasn't actually Cole.

Gabi squirmed her way out from the middle of the group, a look of disgust on her face. "If you ever come to your senses, Cole, and realize how gross she is, come find me."

"Never going to happen," he said.

"We'll see," Gabi replied with an all-knowing, gloating lilt to her voice. Maybe she was in an altered state of mind, but it still was chilling to hear.

The space Gabi left was quickly filled. Everyone wanted to get as close to me as possible. And they all started talking to me at once. Cole, Courtney, other people I knew from school, strangers, everyone. They all had wonderful things to say. But the compliments weren't making me feel good. They were making me feel lousy—especially after what had just happened with Gabi. I just had to reverse that love spell.

Only I couldn't do it on my own. I needed

someone who could actually control their powers at will. I needed Lance Gold. He could fix everything—the love spell, my best friend hating me, my teen parents. He was a major do-gooder. Maybe he would even re-reconsider going out with Gabi.

I had to get back to Lance. After all, weren't guardian angels supposed to help people?

And at that moment, nobody needed more help than me!

chapter

✧ 18 ✧

"Did Lance do his appearance yet?" I asked Cole.

"Who cares?" he said. "You're the only one worth seeing."

"Totally," Reid agreed. Several others echoed that sentiment.

"Cole, come on. I want to know," I said. "Is Lance still here?"

"Yeah, I guess so," he answered, kicking his foot against the ground. "The crowd got a little crazy after you came out onstage. Lance's manager made him stay backstage, and security told us unless everyone simmered down, the event would be canceled. It seemed like they still planned to have it, but most of us didn't care about it anymore. We just wanted to find you." He paused. "Why do you want to see Lance? Do you like him? Better than me?"

"Of course not." It was true. I didn't like Lance better. But at the moment I did need him more than Cole. "We just came here to see him, so I thought we should."

"We'll never get past all that security. Let's do something else instead. Like go to the music store. There's a ton of songs that could have been written just for you."

"Oooh, like Mara's Daughters' 'Mysterious Love,'" Max said.

"Or 'Beautiful Wonder,'" someone else yelled out.

The next thing I knew, everyone was calling out names of songs that reminded them of me.

I couldn't even have a private conversation. Everyone just butted in.

And nothing anyone said was of any importance. Well, other than Cole. He made one good point. We'd never get past all that security around Lance. It was true. There was no way *we* would. But I could.

I just needed to ditch the army following my every move.

"Okay, everyone. I'm so glad you're all here," I said to the crowd. "But I need a little time alone. So why don't we all meet up in the food court in an hour."

"No way," Jaydin said. "What if you take off again? We can't take that chance."

"I promise I won't," I answered her.

"Sorry," some sixth-grader from my school said. "Don't hate us for it. But we're never leaving you. We can't. We love you."

Just perfect. What was I supposed to do?

I turned to Cole. "I need to get away from these people," I whispered.

"What did she say?" Courtney asked.

Cole took my hand. "What she said," he told Courtney and the crowd, "is that this is no way to treat someone as awesome as she is. She wants the royal treatment."

Max started to bow.

"Not like that," Cole said. "What I mean is have a little respect. You all just pounced on her when she arrived. She deserves a grand entrance."

"That's true," Lana agreed. "They play a song when the queen of England enters a room. I bet I can find it on my iPhone."

"Good idea," Cole told her. "There's a Radio Shack right there. Put it on one of their stereos and have everyone wait there. Then Angel can walk in while it plays. And I promise," he crossed his fingers behind his back, "I'll make sure she doesn't disappear."

Lana nodded furiously like she had a new mission in life—to see that I was tended to. "Don't worry, Your Majesty," she assured me. "I'll see to it that everyone gives you the respect you deserve. Come on, people. Don't keep the queen waiting—we have a grand entrance to get ready for." She ushered them to the store.

"Just hide in the bathroom for a little while," Cole told me. "I'll tell them all you ran to the food court. They'll go searching for you there. Then we can duck out of here."

"Perfect," I told Cole.

I slipped into the ladies' room. It was very cool having a smart boyfriend, even one under a spell. Thanks to him, I lost the mob. Or so I thought.

Because next thing I knew I heard him yelling, "You can't go in there!" He was trying to give me a signal that someone was coming into the bathroom. I jumped into a stall, and, as carefully as I could, I placed my feet on the toilet bowl. I stood crouched there praying I wouldn't fall in. Staying still perched on a toilet is a lot harder than it sounds. People in the movies do it all the time, but it was supertough to keep my balance. Especially for someone like me.

It was slippery. I felt one of my feet moving. I tried to stop it, to keep it in place, but I couldn't. It was like it had a mind of its own. And before I knew it, my foot slid right into the toilet bowl! Yuck!

I couldn't even move. I had to keep it there because the door to the bathroom opened. If the water made a splashing noise, whoever it was would find me.

The person was walking around the bathroom. Then I saw her face peer under the stall. It was Jaydin. I froze. *Please don't see me.*

She backed away. Phew. I was free! For a whole second. Because a moment later she shoved the door open. "Gotcha," she said. "I knew Cole was lying. I knew you were just trying to get away."

I should have known not to underestimate Jaydin Salloway. She was way smart.

I jumped off the toilet and ran, my foot squishing water as I went. Why did I always make a bad situation worse? Jaydin was right behind me. Cole, too.

"Angel's over here," Jaydin shouted to everyone in the area. "This way."

I turned into the bookstore and hid behind a shelf.

"You can't get away," Jaydin said. "You're leaving a trail." I looked down. She was right. Toilet-water footprints were leading her right to me.

I wanted to vanish. But seeing as my powers were what got me into this mess, trying another advanced one seemed like a bonehead idea. So I got down on my hands and knees and crawled, trying to stay hidden behind rows of books. As Jaydin and her followers got closer, I crawled under a table in the kids' section and hid.

Jaydin wasn't giving up. That girl was thorough. She looked under every nook and cranny until she spotted me. "Found her," she yelled.

That was all it took. Pretty soon everyone crowded around me in the store. There was no way to get away from these people.

"Sorry," Cole said.

So was I. It royally stunk. Why couldn't these people go back to thinking I was a nobody? Even hating me would be better than this. Then they'd stay away. It was certainly keeping my best friend far from me.

Gabi!

If I was able to make her hate me, I could make *anyone* hate me. Sure, it wasn't the ideal solution. But it beat being shadowed. And it would let me find Lance by myself.

There was no other answer.

It was time to turn my fans against me.

I got out from under the table and yelled at the crowd. "You all hate me!"

"No, we don't," someone shouted back. That was followed by, "We adore you," "You're awesome," and "Angel forever."

"I couldn't hate you," Cole said. "I'll prove it. I'm going to take all of the money I get from my Bar Mitzvah and have the words *I Love You* written in the sky."

A skywriter? Sweet. But no thanks. They needed to stop loving me so much. I closed my eyes and focused. *Stop loving me so much. Stop loving me so much. Stop loving me so much.* But when I peeked through my lashes, everyone was still grinning at me. That wasn't hate. It was awe. They were just as crazy about me as ever.

"Seriously people, listen!" I said.

But they all started chanting. "Angel, Angel, Angel."

If they were all so into me, then why didn't they even pretend to care about what I wanted?

And why weren't my powers working? They had gone off in the dressing room. Maybe because it was quieter in there. There were dozens of people in the bookstore and they were all talking. I just needed to focus more. Tune everyone out.

I jumped on a table and raised my arms as if to engulf everyone around me. I concentrated like my life depended on it. Because it did. If I couldn't get to Lance, then an evil Lou was set loose on the world with no one to stop him. And everyone was in danger. And it would be all my fault! "You don't love me," I said, my voice steady. "You want nothing to do with me." I felt the words run through my body. I imagined everyone turning on me. I pictured it, I felt it, I hoped for it.

"Get off the table," Lana said. "No one wants to look at you."

"Yeah, what are you doing?" Courtney asked. "Posing for the cover of a fashion *don't* book?"

They stopped loving me! My powers had worked!

Maybe too well. Because a book came sailing right at me. People were throwing them in my direction! Even Max who had the biggest crush on me was in on it! I ducked just in time. Three books flew right over my head. But another one followed and got me right in the gut. And it hurt! They couldn't have used a paperback?

"I should have listened to Gabi," Cole said. "She was right about Angel. She's totally gross."

"You're the one who kissed her," Reid said.

"Don't remind me," Cole answered. "Does anyone have one of those hand-sanitizer wipes? I need to disinfect my lips."

It was one thing to hear Courtney sling insults my way, but Cole? It hurt more than twenty books with sharp corners whacking me in the gut.

"You," the saleswoman said, approaching me, "need to leave now." Her face had a huge scowl on it. Bigger than the one Courtney was giving me. And that was saying something.

"Me? I wasn't the one throwing books."

"Doesn't matter. You're not welcome here." She pointed toward the exit. And the rest of the crowd applauded her.

The woman hated me. Just like everyone else in the store.

Which was just as well. Because I had more important things to worry about. Like saving the world from a certain teenager.

chapter

✦ 19 ✦

I forged straight ahead, right out of the store, making sure not to glance back at Cole and the others.

None of it mattered. I just had to get to Lance.

I continued on to the stage area. As I got closer a familiar sound filled the halls. *"Who am I, without you—you, you, who who who?"* Lance Gold was singing! Finally, something was going right. He had begun his mall appearance. Now I didn't have to break in to see him. I could just walk right up to the stage.

"Lance," I called out to him. But he couldn't hear me over the speakers and the cheers from the group that had gathered. I was just another voice in the crowd.

"Lance!" I jumped as high as I could, waving my hands in the air. "It's me, the girl from the backstage area. I need your help. It's important." Still nothing.

Being short was not helping my situation.

How could I get him to notice me? I tried to elbow my way to the front, but no one would let me get through. They just kept bopping up and down to the music. If I stepped left, someone shimmied to the left. If I moved to the right, someone swayed to the right, blocking me. The only way to get to him was to get rid of the crowd. Which meant I had to use my powers.

I closed my eyes. "I need the crowd to leave. To scurry off like little mice." It took hearing myself say the words three times before realizing what an unfortunate word choice I had made. I stopped, but it was too late. I was already feeling fur grazing across my legs. I opened my eyes and sure enough—Mice! Dozens of them scurrying around! How could I have been so stupid as to use a word like *mice* while trying to summon my powers? Hadn't I made enough mistakes to start learning from some of them by now? It was so gross! My mind told me they were people. But my eyes told me they were rodents.

It got worse. When I looked on stage, I hadn't just changed the crowd, I had changed Lance! Where he had been standing, rocking out on a guitar, was now a mouse scurrying up and down the strings of the instrument.

"Why'd you stop playing?" Harmony Gold asked, emerging from backstage. Then she saw all the mice. "What the—," she yelled. She scanned the crowd. That's when she caught sight of me. "You," she said looking me right in the eye.

I waved and gave her a small smile. It was not returned. She was clearly not my biggest fan. A rodent that I'm pretty sure was Lance climbed up her leg. She moved her arm to swat it away.

"No!" I shouted. "It's your son."

"It's my what?" she said, glaring from me to the mouse, stopping her hand mid-swing.

I hoisted myself onto the stage, trying not to squash—or even touch—any rodents. Or their droppings. Then I grabbed Lance. I'd always dreamed of holding him, but not like this. This was gross. He was so squirmy.

Harmony closed her eyes and rubbed her temples. But it didn't seem to be calming her down. Not one bit.

"Angel," she said through clenched teeth. "Give me my son now."

I was a little afraid to hand him over. She went from rubbing her head to wringing her hands together. She looked like she could accidentally squeeze poor Lance to death. "What is going on here?" she asked.

"I was trying to get Lance's attention."

"You got it," she said, dropping her son into the pocket of her blazer.

"I hadn't meant for it to happen this way. I just wanted his help. I know he's a guardian angel . . . and you are, too."

"I don't know what you're talking about." Harmony turned and walked off, careful to avoid stepping on rodents as she left.

"Wait," I yelled after her. "You can't just leave. What about all these people?"

"I don't see any people."

Why was she playing games? Why wouldn't she just admit who she was? "Please. I need your help. I need a guardian angel."

She gave up her charade. "I don't want to get involved," she said, plucking a mouse off Lance's guitar. She took it by the tail and threw it a few feet. It scampered away.

"But I messed up. Big time," I explained. "My powers have been uncontrollable today. First I turned Lou and my moth—"

Harmony cut me off. "It's your mess, Angel. You

116

need to get out of it. I have my own clients to deal with."

I couldn't believe this. What kind of guardian angel was she? She didn't want to help. "Then let me talk to Lance. He'll help. *He's* a nice person. I read about all the good deeds he does."

She looked toward her pocket. "Lance is not in any condition to help anyone."

"But he could be, if you changed him back."

Haromony's eyes got wide. I quickly discovered the cause. A mouse was hanging from the light fixture. And then suddenly it was falling. Right on TOP OF MY HEAD.

I let out a wail and shook my hair like crazy, trying to get the thing out. It was so nasty. "Seriously," I cried, "you're not going to do anything?"

"Okay, fine, I'll help you with your rodent problem," Harmony said, shielding her head from mouse droppings. "But then you need to leave my son and me alone."

"But," I protested, "you don't understand. Lou is on the loose. I changed him—"

She cut me off again. "I don't want to hear it, Angel. If you want my help with the mice, that's my condition."

"Fine," I said. Besides, I didn't need her help with Lou. Once she fixed Lance, I'd get him to help. He was a decent person. He obviously took after his father.

"Now go." She shooed me away like I was one of the rodents.

As I hopped offstage, I saw her place Lance in front of his guitar. Then she snapped her fingers together. The crowd, including her son, morphed back. Little rodent bodies expanded and grew until they were normal-sized, little mouse faces and beady eyes became human ones, and tails and whiskers disappeared until everything was back to the way it was supposed to be. Well, with one exception. People were all over the place. A few were onstage, a couple underneath it, one hanging off the curtain, a few munching on trash from the garbage can.

But Harmony took control. "*You*. Off the stage," she said, pointing at a guy standing in front of her. Probably the same one that had been sniffing at Lance's guitar.

"Come on," she told her son. "What are you doing just standing there? Everyone is waiting for you to play."

Lance looked confused. So did the crowd. They didn't seem to remember being rodents, but they didn't know why they were holding on to empty soda cups and M&M's wrappers. They just stared at Lance as if he'd have an answer.

"Quit joking around," Harmony told Lance. "Start playing."

He did as he was told.

And hopefully, when he was done with his set, he'd do as he was asked—by me.

chapter
20

I watched Lance sing, waiting for his mother to leave. But she was glued to the stage. Probably afraid that I'd try to worm my way back to her son. She was right, of course, but she was making my job a lot more difficult.

I needed help. I needed to create a diversion.

"Look who it is."

I knew that voice. Normally it would have meant help was there. But not this time. This time it meant my best friend was there to torture me.

"Hi, Gabi," I said, turning around.

She was standing next to Cole. How come whenever my powers messed up, it brought my boyfriend and best friend closer together?

"Don't tell me," she said. "You're trying to break in to see Lance again. I'll save you the time. He's not going to want anything to do with you."

For her sake I hoped she was wrong. "I'm going to make everything better," I told her. "Lance is going to love you." Not to mention undo all my mess-ups.

"How many times do I have to tell you?" she yelled. "Stay out of my life."

"Mine too," Cole butted in.

His words put me on the defensive. "Then go! I didn't ask you to come over and bother me. Just leave!"

"We're not going," Gabi answered. "We're here to see Lance. Right, Cole?" She put her hand on his arm as she spoke.

"Right," he said. "If anyone should leave, it's you," he told me.

Gabi nodded in agreement. Then she whispered something in Cole's ear, and they both started laughing. I didn't like Mean Gabi. Nothing was going right. My friends were my enemies, Harmony wouldn't help me, and I couldn't get close to Lance on my own.

Which was exactly what I was—on my own.

chapter

✦ 21 ✦

I couldn't watch Gabi and Cole for one more second, so I left and wandered the mall. My nails were practically nonexistent. I had chewed them as low as they could possibly go, and I still hadn't come up with a way to get to see Lance.

"Bull's-eye," Lana called out as a french fry bounced off my head. At least it wasn't a mouse.

"Big deal," Jaydin answered. "Her head is ginormous. There was no way you could have missed. Now if you had managed to hit her boobs, that would have been impressive. They practically don't even exist."

So much for leaving me alone. I had wound up in the food court with a slew of my haters ready to bring on the ridicule.

More fries came at me.

"Told you that you wouldn't hit the target," Jaydin said.

"I can't believe I wasted my fries on her," Lana complained. The two wandered off, going on and on about how it was all my fault that they were going to be hungry now.

"You are the strangest girl I know," a voice called out to me.

I turned around. It was D.L. He was sitting about three tables back in front of the McDonald's.

Just what I needed, another run-in with someone under the hate spell.

I didn't bother to answer. I walked in the other direction.

"Hey," D.L. called after me. "Where are you going?"

"I don't have time to listen to you harass me," I answered.

"Whoa," he said. "Can't you take a joke? I didn't mean anything by it."

That was odd. D.L. didn't seem overly disgusted with me.

"I swear," he said. "This Lance thing has everyone acting crazy. Courtney just stormed off because I didn't *understand*"—he made little air quotes with his fingers—"how much getting Lance's autograph mattered." He dropped the quotes. "Who cares? He's just a guy. And I'm way hotter, anyway."

I was taken aback. And not because D.L. was so shallow. But because he was acting just like D.L.

And like he was completely unaffected by the powers!

chapter
✦ 22 ✦

D.L. just kept talking—not really caring if I was listening or not. "Courtney said she wanted an autograph, so I signed my name on a napkin. She didn't even smile. I mean, seriously, that was funny. She didn't say it had to be Lance's. But she just crumpled it up and threw it at me."

D.L. was treating me strangely. Actually, he was treating me normally, which at that very moment was kind of strange. "Don't you hate me?" I asked, taking a seat across from him.

"Well . . . ," he said, shaking his hand in a back and forth gesture—signaling it was fifty-fifty. But then he broke into a huge grin and looked right at me. His eyes were even dancing.

Oh no! That smile. That look! I knew what they meant. I had seen them before—by a mob of obsessed

Angel fans. D.L. was under the love spell. He was giving me an I-think-you-are-the-only-one-for-me smile. "Not you, too. I can't handle another person crushing on me."

He almost spit out the soda he had gulped down. "Did you seriously just say that?"

I felt my face turning hot. "I was just kidding." How *could* I have said that?

"I was JOKING," I said.

"Some sense of humor," he said through hiccups of laughter. Not that I could blame him. Talk about embarrassing.

"People have been acting weird around me today. You saw it," I said, trying to justify why I'd made a total fool of myself.

The more I squirmed, the more he chuckled.

"Yeah, hardy har," I said. "Angel says something ridiculous again. I'm sure you and Courtney will have a great big laugh over it."

D.L. ran his fingers through his hair and his face lost the smile. "Courtney and I aren't laughing over anything. She's been acting crazy. I was sitting here minding my own business, and she screamed at me for not caring about things that are important to her. Things like Lance." He said the name *Lance* the way

126

you'd say the word *poo*. "Why should I have to watch her go crazy over some other guy? I came to the mall, isn't that enough?"

Duh! Of course. I should have known. D.L. wasn't infected by the love spell because he wasn't near the stage when it went off. Same for the hate rush I sent toward everyone in the bookstore. He had been at the food court the whole time—far away from dangerous old me.

"Nothing's ever enough for Courtney. She's a pain in the—," I stopped myself. D.L. was the only person who I could actually talk to right now. The only friend, well, sort-of friend, who wasn't impaired by some spell I had cast over them. I didn't want to mess it up by insulting his girlfriend. "She'll get over it."

"I don't know." He shook his head and his floppy hair swayed back and forth. "She was pretty steamed."

"Why do you even care? It doesn't sound like you even like her."

He shrugged his shoulder. "She's hot."

Uck. Boys. Figured that was his answer. "There are a lot of girls who are hot *and* nice. Like Gabi."

"She's no Courtney," he said.

That got me mad. Until I realized that maybe it was a good thing. *Maybe* D.L.'s feelings for Courtney were just what I needed to get to Lance.

It was worth a shot.

"What if I told you I knew how you could make it up to Courtney?" I asked. "How you could make her crazy happy?"

He raised an eyebrow at me. "I'm listening."

"I'm planning to sneak backstage to see Lance once his appearance is over. Help me get in, and I'll get him to make out an autograph for her. When you give it to her, you'll look like a hero."

The corner of his mouth raised into a half smile and he nodded his head. I knew he was picturing Courtney hanging all over him after he handed her the signed photo. Prince Charming saving the day for his beautiful, cruel princess.

"Well?" I asked him.

"I'm in," he said.

D.L. was going to be more of a hero than he could have imagined.

"I do have to warn you," I told him. "There is a chance you might get in a *little* bit"—I held my hands out wide to show that I actually meant a lot—"of trouble."

128

D.L. smiled. "What else is new?" I had forgotten for a second that D.L. was a troublemaker.

Exactly what I needed in someone to help me pull off my scheme.

chapter
✦ 23 ✦

As D.L. and I headed back toward Lance, I filled him in on what I wanted him to do. He was going to be my decoy.

We were halfway there when we bumped into Reid.

"Check this out!" Reid reached into his backpack, pulled out a baseball, and tossed it at D.L.

"Yeah, so?" D.L. asked.

"Look what's written on it."

It had Babe Ruth's signature on it. "What? Did you sign it yourself?" D.L. asked.

"Nope," Reid said. "It's the genuine thing. You can keep it, if you want."

D.L. scrutinized the ball. "Why would you give me this? It's worth a fortune."

Reid patted his bag. "Because I can have as many as I want."

"What are you talking about?" I asked, even though I was a little afraid of the answer. This seemed to have Lou written all over it. "Where'd you get that?"

Reid glared down at me. "Why would I tell you?"

I had forgotten that Reid was among those who hated me now.

I nudged D.L.

"Yeah," he said, finally opening his mouth. "How can you get as many as you want?"

Reid glared at me and crossed his arms.

"Come on, dude. Spill," D.L. pushed, still gripping the ball.

Reid took D.L. by the arm and moved him three feet away. "Fine. But don't tell her," he said.

Luckily, he wasn't as good a whisperer as he thought.

"Down by the Apple store. It's like the craziest thing," Reid explained. "This girl started talking to me. Then all of a sudden a guy butted in. He wanted me to get lost. It wasn't like I was doing anything. I like Lana, but he was all jealous, anyway. So he said he'd make it worth my while if I left. That he could grant me a wish. I didn't believe it. But I figured why not. So I wished for a magic bag—for anything I want

131

to show up right in my backpack. And it actually worked!"

No, no, no, no! Reid must have run into Lou and my mother.

"No way," D.L. said. "A magic bag? Get real."

"I'm serious," Reid said. "It works."

D.L. shook his head and tossed the ball back at Reid. "Dude, you've been played. There's no such thing as a magic bag. I can't believe you fell for something like that. Did they sell you the Empire State Building, too?"

"This is real," Reid said. "This bag can give me anything I want. Well, anything that fits inside it."

D.L. crossed his arms in front of him. "Then prove it."

"All right," Reid said, his eyes lighting up. He reminded me of one of the guys on those early morning infomercials that try to sell you their amazing steak knives.

"A pint of Ben & Jerry's Chubby Hubby, presto." Reid pulled out a container from his bag. "Gold coins, alakazam." He reached in and came out with a handful of gold coins. "Games for my Wii, abracadabra!" And suddenly he was holding Wii Sports Resort and the new Super Mario Bros. game.

"No way," D.L. said, grabbing the bag.

"It's true," Reid said.

"I want signed baseball cards," D.L. said. He looked inside the bag. "See, I knew it wouldn't work."

"Of course not for *you*," Reid said. "It's *my* magic bag." Reid closed his eyes. "Signed baseball cards," he intoned. Seconds later, he reached inside and pulled them out.

D.L.'s eyes practically popped out of their sockets.

I couldn't keep quiet any longer. "Don't tell me, you got the bag from a guy with big dimples, right? Did you have to sign anything? Make a trade? People don't give you stuff for nothing." It sounded like Lou just didn't want Reid flirting with Mom, but I had a feeling that wasn't the only reason. Young Lou wanted to control the world. What better way than collecting tons of souls?

"Wasn't talking to you," Reid said.

"She does have a point," D.L. interjected. He was still examining the backpack, looking for a reasonable explanation for Reid's magic bag. "What did it cost?"

"That's the best part! Absolutely nothing."

"And you believed that?" I asked.

He sneered at me. "I'm not stupid. The guy said I'd be helping him with his documentary, *Sold Out*, about giving away his fortune and making people's dreams come true. I just had to sign a waiver."

"Did you even read it?" I yelled. The idiot had probably just traded away his soul and didn't even realize it. Chances were it wasn't a waiver to be in a documentary. It was a waiver of any rights he had to his life. A written agreement to spend eternity in the underworld. I had a feeling Lou's fake documentary wasn't called Sold *Out*, but rather Soul*ed Out*. Meaning he was getting people to sell him their souls.

"You need to give back the wish."

Reid's eyebrows furrowed. "No way. Do you see this? It's the real deal. And I was smart. I didn't just get one thing," he said, tapping his head. "I made it so I can get unlimited gifts. Cash, a new baseball glove, an iPad, anything that fits in my backpack is mine." He then opened his bag and proceeded to pull out cash, a baseball glove, and an iPad.

"Maybe we should check out what this wish thing is all about," D.L. said, still keeping a hand on Reid's bag. "Then I won't need a stupid autograph. I can make Courtney crazy for me without i—"

"No!" I interrupted, and pulled D.L.'s hand off

Reid's bag. "Love spells are awful. You don't want someone to like you because of that. Trust me."

"How would you know?" D.L. asked.

"Umm," I stammered. "It's obvious. You'd never know for sure if the person really likes you."

There was no way I was letting D.L. make a deal with my father. The price was too high. Besides, Courtney certainly wasn't risk-your-soul hot.

"Fine," D.L. said. "Then forget the love spell. There are tons of other things I could wish for. I wouldn't mind my own magic bag."

"This whole thing doesn't sound too good to be true to you?" I asked. "Don't you think there's a catch?"

"Sorry," Reid said to D.L. "I'm outta here. I've had enough. *She*"—he pointed to me—"is such a downer. I can't stand to be around her. Just the sight of her makes me wish I had asked for an Angel-free world."

Which reminded me . . . I had a real angel I needed to get to.

"But did you see all that stuff he had?" D.L. gestured to Reid as he walked off. "That bag was empty and he pulled out an iPad. You can't fake that."

"Yes, you can. Haven't you ever heard of the magic of Hollywood?" I argued. "There could have been an extra compartment in his bag that you never found.

Or maybe Reid is a great magician and used sleight of hand to make it look like those things came from the bag. They were probably under his sweater. This could all be a big setup. A documentary on how people are gullible—and Reid is in on it. Now, are we getting the autograph for Courtney or do you want to go make a joke of yourself? I'm sure your girlfriend won't want to see you made a fool of on some show."

"All right," D.L. said, giving in. "Let's go."

It was about time!

chapter 24

We got to the stage area, and everyone was gone. Everyone but security. The concert was over.

"Ready?" I asked D.L.

"Ready," he answered.

And just like that D.L. ran up to the guards and tried to push his way into the backstage area. It felt like we were in a movie. One where we were about to save the world. James Bond, watch out.

"You can't go in there," the bigger guard told him.

"Try and stop me," D.L. answered.

The skinny one tried to do just that. He reached for D.L.'s arm, but D.L. ran. The guy was fast. He raced around the corner with the first guard chasing him. A second later D.L. was back at the door trying to get inside again. This time the second guard tried to catch him. Before I knew it, D.L. had both men following him, and when he turned the corner, the coast was clear for me to get backstage. I booked it to the door before the guards could make it back.

Once I made it inside, I kept my eyes glued on the door to make sure I wasn't followed. But when you're looking backward, you can't really see what's in front of you. And that's how I smashed right into Lance Gold.

"You again," he said, backing up from me. He ended up wedging himself against the wall where Clothes Therapy used to keep the shoes. Which worked for me. I had him cornered.

The best part was that I didn't see his mother. That was a good sign. Hopefully, she would stay wherever she was for a long, long time.

"Yup. It's me. The one who tried to fix you up with the world's most amazing girl. But that's not why I'm here now."

I didn't care that he didn't look excited to see me. I delved right into my plea. "I need your help," I said in an almost whisper out of the side of my mouth. "I made a mess of things and now the devil is out there hurting innocent people."

Lance didn't say anything. "Don't worry," I assured him. "I know who you really are. I know you have powers."

"What?" he asked, looking at me like I'd escaped from the insane asylum. "What do you mean *powers*? I played a superhero in one of my movies, but that was make-believe. It's called acting."

"It's okay—your secret's safe with me. I've got powers, too," I told him.

Just then, his mother threw open the office door. "Lance," she said, joining him, "go wait in the back room."

"I'm not leaving you alone with her," he said. "She might be dangerous."

Oh my gosh. He thought I was like my father. That I'd actually hurt his mom. "I won't hurt her. I'm not the devil."

Lance looked kind of frightened.

"LANCE. NOW!" his mother said.

"But—," he protested.

"GO!"

He did as he was told. It was just me and Harmony Gold face-to-face. Again.

"I told you to leave us alone."

"I'm sorry," I said. "I don't want to cause any trouble. I just need help. And I thought maybe Lance would be more understanding than you.

139

He's always doing stuff for others. And what I'm asking would help tons of innocent people."

"Keep my son out of this." She tried to usher me out, but I wouldn't let her.

"No. If you won't help me, maybe he will." I was hoping I'd have better luck with someone closer to my age who understood what it was like dealing with a difficult parent.

Harmony let out a long sigh. "Lance can't help you undo anything," she said, her hands on her hips. "You may know his secret, but he doesn't. He has no clue that he comes from angels. And that's exactly how I intend it to stay."

He didn't know? No wonder he was so scared of me. I must have seemed like a lunatic to him. Okay, I could deal with this. It was just a minor curveball. "Then, please, can't you help me?" I begged her. "I made it so Lou thinks he's a teen again. And I think you know what happened during that point in his life."

Harmony closed her eyes for a second. She took a deep breath before speaking. "I do. But there's a pact in place. I don't mess with Lou. He doesn't mess with me."

"But when did you make that? Probably not when he was all wicked and trying to take over the planet.

And that's where he is now. So the pact doesn't count."

"Sorry, Angel. A deal is a deal."

Sorry? She was going to let the world suffer at the hands of Lucifer and all she could give me was *sorry*?

"Fine," I said. "If you don't help me, then I'll just tell Lance the truth about his identity."

Was I actually blackmailing an angel? I was going to need a serious karma-cleansing after this was over. "I bet Lance has powers, too," I went on. "Even if he hasn't activated them yet." I looked her right in the eyes, daring her to test me.

"You would never do that," she said. "It's not your place and you know it."

"All I know is that I need to stop Lou."

"But you won't do it this way. You won't tell Lance his true identity. Because you're good. Truly good. And you understand that he needs to be told in the right way at the right time."

Wow. So Harmony Gold thought I was good. That was kind of a big deal. I mean, if anyone's a good judge of character, it would have to be an angel. Still, good wasn't enough to get the job done.

"I can't stop Lou myself. I wouldn't ask for help if I didn't need to."

She shook her head no.

"But I have no one. Everyone's under a stupid spell."

"Ahh," she said, "that's right. I sent your powers back at you. Some of my better work, I must say. It's my 'I'm Rubber, You're Glue' shield. I invented that one when I was about your age. I'll tell you what, I'll help you undo the love spell, since I did partially create that situation to begin with."

Sort of? Try definitely. But I wasn't going to complain. At least she'd agreed to do something. Only I had already undone the love spell. For a whole chunk of people, anyway. "It's a little more complicated now," I confessed. "I tried to fix it myself and made a group of people feel hate for me instead."

She shook her head. "You need to sharpen your focus. You kids today, you're just not ready for your powers. If it were up to me, you'd all wait until you were eighteen to find out about your special gifts . . . not just Lance." She waved her arm in the air, as if swatting away a major annoyance—namely me. "All right, let's undo both spells together."

I nodded. We took each other's hands. I bet it would have looked weird to anyone who knew our secrets. An angel and the devil's kid working together to fix a problem.

"Now focus," she said. "Concentrate on reversing

the hate spell. I'll concentrate on removing the love spell. Everyone will be back to normal in no time."

Except for anyone who dared cross my father's path. But I blocked that out of my mind. One problem at a time.

I did as Harmony instructed. Two minutes later she dropped my hands. "All fixed," she said.

But we both knew better. There was a lot more that needed to be repaired.

chapter
✦ 25 ✦

"'K, bye," I said, heading toward the door.

"Yeah, see ya," she said, rather anxious to get rid of me.

I knew she wanted me to go, and I wanted to go, but I couldn't. My feet wouldn't move. I was stuck there, frozen with fear.

"I said good-bye, Angel."

"I know," I answered, "I'm trying to go."

Apparently I wasn't trying hard enough for her, because, the next thing I knew, she had lifted me up and had carried me to the exit. The woman was strong.

She was literally shoving me out the door.

"Wait," I said, holding on to the doorframe as she tried to pry my fingers away. "What am I going to do to stop Lou?"

"You know how. It's within you."

Wait a minute. That was it? That was her big advice? That didn't help me at all. If I knew, I wouldn't have asked! She was just trying to get rid of me. "You have to give me more than that." I held on to the doorframe for dear life.

"Now I wouldn't be a very good guardian angel if I just went around giving out answers, would I?" she asked. She kept pushing me out of the room. But I was strong, too. "I'm supposed to guide people to figure out their own solutions, not give them answers."

We weren't talking small everyday problems, like whether to use toothpaste or pimple cream to get rid of a zit. Or what shirt makes muffin tops look less noticeable. We were talking huge, possible destruction-of-life-as-we-know-it problems. I thought she'd make an exception.

"But this is major. I'm not trying to get my allowance raised, I'm trying—"

She didn't let me get any further. "I told you, I'm not getting involved with the devil. This is your problem to solve. Now don't even try coming back here. Once you leave, I'm putting a protective spell around this area. No one will be able to break inside. No powers, either. And I'm leaving it up until you can get through to Lou."

145

"And what if I can't?" Only two of my fingers were left clutching the door. I couldn't hold on much longer. But I didn't want to go out there. Not alone. Not without her backing me up.

"Just trust in yourself, Angel."

That was one thing I couldn't do. This was way over my head. How could I go up against my own father? I was a newbie. I wasn't equipped to battle the king of all things evil. "Lou against me is the same as a giant going up against an ant."

"Ants are stronger than you think." And on that note she gave one final shove, pushing me completely outside. Then she slammed the door shut. I certainly didn't feel very strong.

I wandered a few yards. And there, sitting at a table with security, was D.L.! I had forgotten all about him.

"Are you okay?" I asked.

He shrugged. "Did you get the autograph?"

I had completely forgotten. I hadn't even asked.

"You," a guard I hadn't seen before said to me, saving me from D.L.'s question. "You need to leave."

"But what about him?"

"Don't worry about him."

I had to do *something*.

"I just came out of there," I said. "You had to have

seen me! I left my phone inside. I just need it back. Please!"

He didn't say anything.

I tugged at his sleeve. "If I lose that phone my parents will kill me. It will just be a second. I promise."

"Fine," he said and knocked on the door.

Finally something was going my way. I'd get D.L. off the hook, get him his photo, and then deal with the real issues.

Only no one answered the knock. And when the guard tried to open the door, it wouldn't budge. Harmony's protection power. There was no way in. Not until I took care of Lou.

D.L. was going to have to wait.

chapter

✦ 26 ✦

A loud blast went off at the other side of the mall, followed by screams. Dozens of them!

I followed the shouts, and, for the umpteenth time that day, I ran across the mall.

I pictured Lou doing awful things—engulfing people in flames, chaining them to gumball machines, making them clean the floor with their tongues. But that wasn't what I found at all. In fact, it was the opposite. People were screaming out of excitement. Hundred-dollar bills were shooting out from a hole in the ceiling. All the shoppers were fighting to grab as many of the bills as they could. And standing right in the middle of the cash-covered floor were Lou and my mother.

"What's going on here?" I asked them.

Lou looked away and Mom chuckled. "Well, it

seems," she said, playing with a button on Lou's shirt, "that he'll do just about anything to make sure no one talks to me."

"Not true," Lou said. But the blush rising in his cheeks told me it was. "They were just annoying me. All here to see stupid Lance Gold. So I gave them something better. Money."

"Well, I still want to meet Lance," Mom said. "That's why I picked coming to the mall in the first place." My mother was totally boy-crazed.

"You don't need to meet him," Lou said. "Look," he waved his arm and everyone around us froze. "Isn't this better? Peace and quiet. The whole mall is yours. How often does that happen? You can shop for as long as you want. Have whatever you want."

"Anything?" she asked.

"Anything," he repeated.

"And no one will bug us?"

"Nope," he said.

"What about her?" she asked. "Why is she here? Didn't you tell her to stay at the house?"

"I can send her back," he offered.

"NO," I shouted and grabbed onto his arm. "Please don't. I'm your"—I almost forgot about that

149

little lie I had told him—"*sister*. I just want to hang out a little." He looked to my mom.

"Fine," she said, "as long as she doesn't get in my way. It's *my* mall today."

"She won't," Lou said.

Then he snapped his fingers, and I was no longer standing next to my parents. Instead I was standing inside a big turtle-shaped sandbox. Surrounded by three tricycles, an orange plastic slide, four frozen toddlers, two adults, and encircled by a gated fence. Lou had sent me to mall day care!

The nerve! At least I wasn't frozen. But I was on the *way* opposite side of the mall. I needed to get back to Lou. Talk some sense into him. I was so tired of running. I looked at the tricycle. Could I? Should I?

I did.

Thank goodness no one could see me. I looked like a clown at the circus, riding a too-small-for-her bike. I was the perfect punch line for any of Courtney's jokes.

I pedaled down the hallway back toward the east wing of the mall where I had last seen my parents. But there was no guarantee they were still there. Lou could flash anywhere in a millisecond. I rode past the security booth and stopped short.

I had an idea. I ditched the tricycle and squeezed

inside the booth. The frozen guard was taking up a lot of space, so I tried to push him aside. I needed access to his monitors. Control of the whole mall was at his fingertips. And now it was at mine.

With each button I pushed, different areas of the mall flashed on-screen. I saw D.L. at the desk near the stage, Porter hunched over the air-hockey table, Courtney mid-hair flip at the food court about to pay the cashier for her drink. But no sign of my parents. I just kept pushing buttons. And then I saw them. At Bloomingdale's. Lou was carrying a huge pile of clothes and Mom just kept flinging more onto it.

At least I knew where to find them. But I needed a new set of wheels. I grabbed the guard's keys and hopped into his mini security go-kart. I had never driven before, except for bumper cars, but this couldn't be that different. And I certainly had watched enough movies to figure out how to start a car.

I put the key in the ignition and got a little rush as the engine started. Then I pushed down on the gas pedal and before I knew it, I was whizzing past store after store. The Gap and H&M on my right, Pacific Sunwear on my left, and, fast-approaching, was a jewelry kiosk right where my go-kart was headed. I tried to swerve, but I wasn't quite there yet with my driving, and I smashed straight into it.

Luckily, I didn't knock it over, but there was jewelry everywhere. There wasn't any time to spare so, instead of cleaning up, I just kept going.

I passed the food court. And Courtney. She had a soda can in her hand. I grabbed it and kept driving. I deserved a beverage.

Then I passed a soft-serve machine that was calling out to me. So I just put my mouth underneath the spout, pulled the lever, and let the ice cream drip straight in. It was like a dream come true!

When I passed the music store, I saw a frozen Cole and Gabi. They were sharing headphones, listening to something. I went right inside and looked to see what was playing. Some sappy Mara's Daughters love song!

No way. Not on my watch.

I took the headphones off of Gabi's head and pulled her to her own station. She seemed to weigh a lot more frozen. But the floor was slippery, so I was able to slide her most of the way. Then I went back to Cole. I had to change his song selection. I did a search for the word *angel*. Something by Jimi Hendrix came up. I wasn't quite sure who he was, but I didn't care. As long as the name Angel was pumping into Cole's head, I was happy. He needed to think about me.

I raced back to my go-kart and drove right into Bloomingdale's to the teen section where I had seen my mom. She wasn't there. But I could tell she had been. Clothes were strewn all over the place.

I drove past the shoes and the purses, basically following a trail of destruction. I finally spotted her and Lou at the perfume counters. I parked and moved in closer to hear what they were saying.

"What do you think?" Mom asked him, misting one fragrance into the air. "Like this one?"

"Nice," Lou said.

"*Nice?* I want better than nice. Maybe this one then?" Mom questioned, picking up a different perfume. This one she sprayed on her wrist and ran it under Lou's nose.

"Mmm," he said.

"That's better," Mom answered. "I wonder if Lance will like it, too." She was totally taunting Lou—trying to make him jealous.

"Why do you care about him?" Lou asked, dropping Mom's bundles of clothes onto the counter. "I'm the one with powers. He's nothing special."

"Nothing special?" Mom said. "Everyone is in

this mall because they came to see him. That makes him pretty powerful in my book. How many people are here to see you?" Her voice was teasing, but Lou wasn't laughing.

"You want to see how many?" he asked. "Just watch. Remember that guy I granted the wish for? The one who wanted the magic bag? The one you were being all flirty with? Well, I'll do the same thing for the whole mall. Grant them all wishes. Then they'll be begging for *my* attention. And every single one of their souls will be mine. Then you'll see who's all-powerful." He stormed out of the store.

I cringed. I did not like where this was going.

I followed him out. Lou waved his hand toward the wall. Moments later, a sign was emblazoned there. A sign encircled with flames. It said MAKE A WISH.

Then he snapped again and everyone came back to life. "Step right up," Lou called to everyone around. "It's your chance of a lifetime. Star in a documentary where I make your wish come true. Whatever you want. Yours for the asking. Step right up."

Now, me personally, if I had seen a sign made of fire and a man offering me my heart's desire, I'd have been spooked.

Apparently I would have been in the minority.

Because Reid wasn't the only one dumb enough to fall for my father's claims. A line immediately started forming. It even rounded the corner. People were jumping at the chance to have Lou make their dreams come true. To be in his documentary. To be "soul-ed out."

I didn't know what to do. My body just stood there motionless as the first man walked up to Lou.

"I want to win the lottery," the guy said.

"No problem," Lou answered, patting him on the back. "Just sign the waiver."

The man took the pen. He didn't even read what he was signing. I'm sure at the bottom in very small print was wording that gave away his soul.

Although, I have to admit, I've done that, too. Not given away my soul, but signed without reading. All those computer games. They have a million rules and regulations. I never bother to look at them all. If I survived today, that was going to change.

"So these are really the winning numbers?" the man asked, clutching onto a lotto ticket.

"That's right," Lou said. "After tonight you'll be a mega-millionaire."

"I guess I don't lose anything either way," the guy said, stuffing the ticket into his pocket.

He was definitely wrong. He just lost big time.

"Next," Lou said with a sweeping gesture.

Max shuffled up to my father.

Not Max! If anyone's soul didn't belong in the underworld, it was Max Richardson's. Even if he *had* thrown a book at me. How was I supposed to stop this?

"And what can I do for you?" Lou asked Max. "What's your secret desire? Your biggest wish? Anything you want is yours!"

Max swayed back and forth on his feet and looked down. "Well . . . ," he said.

"Go on," Lou pressed.

"Well, I wish Angel would love me."

"NO!" I screamed. "Wait. Don't grant that."

The love spell was supposed to be over. No one was supposed to be crazy in love with me anymore or care what I thought about them. I looked around at the crowd. None of them did. None of them even noticed I was there.

No! This wasn't the result of powers, this was the result of Max's monster crush. "Max," I pleaded, "this is not what you want. You were just joking, right?"

Max couldn't even look at me and his shoulders slumped more than usual. "But you must hate me after everything I said to you today. I need to fix that."

"I don't hate you," I told him.

"But I threw a book at you before!" he screamed. "I don't even know why I did it. There's no way you'd ever like me now . . ." His voice trailed off.

"It's okay," I said. "I forgive you."

"She's probably just saying that," Lou said. "I'd sign the waiver and make the wish just to be safe."

Some dad.

"Lou, can we talk for a second?" I said. I wanted to take his arm and drag him off. But I was afraid to touch him. He might have sliced off my hand.

"What?" he asked, stepping a few feet away from Max.

"Don't do this to me. I'm your sister. You don't want your sister under a love spell."

"A wish is a wish," he said. "What do I care?"

"Because I have powers, too. And if I'm under a spell, who knows what I'd do in the name of Max? Maybe I'd try to make him the ruler of the underworld."

"Then I'd just undo it. You barely know how to use your powers. You're not much of a threat. Besides, even with powers, that kid could never beat me."

We both looked at Max. He had both of his hands covering his face, and he was shaking his head back and forth. Lou had a point.

157

"Maybe not. But why would you want the extra headache? Wouldn't it just be simpler to ignore his wish? Come on," I pleaded. "Do it for your favorite sister." I gave him a big smile.

"Fine," he relented. "If it means not having to deal with you anymore then I won't grant it." He rolled his eyes. "You're quite a pain."

Huh . . . I had to admit, I was surprised by how much Lou's words bothered me. Lou never got fed up with me before. He liked having me around.

"All right, kid," Lou said, moving back to Max. "Make another wish. Nothing to do with her."

"Umm," Max said, making sure not to look in my direction. His face was pretty red. "How about I never have to go to school again, and I get paid millions to play video games all day."

"No problem," Lou handed him a pen. "Just sign the waiver."

"Don't do it, Max," I said, pushing his hand away.

Lou glared at me, but I didn't care. This was Max. I didn't want to date him, but that didn't mean I didn't care about him.

"But I want to stay home from school, and I love video games," he mumbled.

"Well," I answered. "You say you love me, too, right? But if you really do, you won't sign that paper. If you care about me at all, you'll just walk away. Go home."

Max's face got redder as he glanced from Lou to me. His expression was a combination of embarrassment and feeling torn.

"Don't listen to her," Lou said. "She's doesn't even like you. She doesn't care about what's best for you."

"That's not true, Max. Please go." I grabbed his hand and squeezed it.

His mouth fell open a little as he looked at my fingers over his.

"Please," I said again.

He nodded. "Oh . . . okay . . ." He handed Lou his pen and turned and left.

Thank God.

One soul saved. One zillion more to go.

chapter

✦ 27 ✦

"Don't you ever interfere with one of my deals again. Do you understand me? I've been very nice to you, but I'm getting tired of it. I have important work to do." Lou's normally light eyes turned pitch-black.

I stood my ground. "What you're doing isn't right. This isn't you—not anymore." Even if Lou still wasn't perfect, he was better than the guy standing in front of me now.

"You don't know anything about me. I never even met you until this morning."

His memory lapse was more than annoying. It was dangerous. "Fine. You're right. But these people at the mall, you don't want their souls. Don't you want scary, evil people? These guys are good." At least I figured they were. Most of them anyway.

"I'll take any soul I can get. I'm going to build up

my team—make the underworld a powerful place. Show everyone"—he looked toward the store where he had left my mom—"how no one can compare to me. It's going to be awe-inspiring."

The sound of his voice, the excitement there, I had never heard him so happy. Not even when I said I'd let him in my life.

"I need a huge team, masses of people to do whatever I want," Lou went on.

"This is crazy," I said.

"No." He shook his head. "This is fun. And it's just the beginning."

Lou loved his life. He loved what he was doing. How did you talk someone out of following their dream? Even if it's a demented dream.

"Make a wish. Just get in line." That voice caught my attention. Not just because it was recruiting people for the devil. But because it was my mother's.

"Mom!" I called out. But she didn't even look my way. Which made sense. She didn't consider herself a mother. "Tammi . . . I mean Maggie," I called out.

She guided people out of Bloomingdale's and toward the end of the line. Then she made her way over to me. Well, over to Lou, to be exact.

She winked at my father. "I decided to help you."

"Maggie!" I shrieked.

"What?" She flipped her hair over her shoulder, then gave me an annoyed look.

"What?" I repeated. "How can you help him?" I wanted to shake her.

"Why wouldn't I? His powers can do incredible things."

"Sure. But at what price?"

She rolled her eyes at me. ROLLED her eyes! "Will you lighten up? It's not hurting anyone."

"Are you kidding me?" I yelled. "It's hurting them all. He's taking their souls."

"Whatever," she said. "He's giving them what they want, why shouldn't he get something in return?"

Was this really my mother? The same woman who made sweetness serums? Who cleansed auras? Whose best friend was the third face on her totem pole that warded off evil spirits? She wouldn't help the devil hurt people. Not knowingly. She had to have thought the soul thing was a joke. If she needed me to spell it out for her, I would.

"Mo—Maggie, have you forgotten that Lou is the devil?"

She winked at him. "I remember."

Okay, I knew Lou had used some hocus-pocus

162

to make her understanding of powers and the supernatural, but this was *too* understanding.

Mom smiled at Lou. "I think it's kind of hot."

It was *me* who had forgotten. *This* Mom liked bad boys.

"And y'know," she said, "it doesn't mean he's evil. He's nicer to me than my so-called friends. You should have seen what happened to me during cheerleading practice yesterday."

Mom had been a cheerleader? She never told me that.

"Kristin Temblin intentionally dropped me from the top of the pyramid. I fell right in a big puddle of mud. And instead of rushing to my side, everyone laughed. Hello! I know Kristin did it on purpose, too. She was just mad that I told her she was too fat to be on the top. Plus she's always been jealous of me. I can't help it if all the boys like me best."

Oh. My. God. My mom was Courtney Lourde.

The woman who raised me would have been the same girl who tortured me in the lunch room if we had been classmates.

"I have an idea!" Mom clapped her hands together and turned to Lou. "I can totally pay Kristin back—with your help! Give her a face full of zits. Make

163

her break out into the hokey-pokey anytime someone says her name. Or better yet oink like a pig. Will you help me?" She batted her eyelashes at Lou.

"Anything for you," Lou said, grinning at her. "If it's Kristin you want, it's Kristin you'll get."

A moment later there was a cloud of smoke. As it evaporated, I could see a woman standing in its place.

A woman who slouched a little. And wore clothes one size too big. One I could only imagine was someone my mother had loved to torture back in the day. Someone who hadn't done anything to deserve getting messed with but became a target, anyway. Someone just like me.

chapter

✧ 28 ✧

"Who is that?" My mom practically stamped her
foot in a hissy fit. "It's certainly not Kristin."

"That's not possible," Lou said. "I don't mess up."

"Well it's not her!" Mom jutted out her bottom lip
in a pout.

"How did I get here?" the woman asked, stumbling.
She didn't know which way to turn. When her eyes
settled on my mother, her face scrunched up. "Maggie?"
The woman shook her head. "Can't be," she mumbled
to herself. "Are you Margaret's daughter?"

"Okay? *Daughter?* What is with everyone today?
And how do you know me?" Mom asked.

Oh no! The woman recognized Mom. It *was* Kristin.
But not the Kristin my mom was talking about. This
Kristin was the adult version of her. This Kristin was
Mom's real age. This woman was old.

Kristin grabbed her wrist and squeezed. "I must be hallucinating. This is insane. I was just at my daughter's soccer game. Maybe it's heatstroke. Snap out of it, Kristin. Wake up. Wake up. Wake up."

The woman was losing it.

"Go that way!" I told her and pointed down the hall. "Go to the food court, get out of here. Now."

She stood there frozen.

"I mean it, go!" I said, sounding like Harmony Gold when she was trying to get Lance away from me. I gave her a push. She didn't budge. "You're dreaming," I lied. "And you won't wake up until you finish what you need to do. And what you need to do is go to the food court."

"Why?"

Because it was far away from my parents. But I couldn't tell her that. "There's a man who works at Subway and he has a majorly important message for you from the future. That's all I know. Now go!"

"But I don't believe in fortune-telling and magic," she said.

"This is a dream, remember?" I told her. "Now go, and don't come back here."

Kristin took one more glance at me and my mother and headed down the hallway.

166

But as I got rid of one person I didn't want near the devil and his new partner in crime, I gained two new ones in their place . . .

"Angel!"

It was Cole, and Gabi was with him.

"We've been looking everywhere for you," he said as they both ran up to me.

Hmmm. If looking very hard meant listening to mushy love songs. They weren't searching. But I was going to give them the benefit of the doubt. Maybe they had just stopped for a break. I mean, I had stopped for a soda and ice cream.

"When I saw the sign, I figured you'd be close by," Gabi continued. "I know how much you like wishes." She definitely added that last part in for Cole's benefit. She didn't want to clue him in that I had anything to do with this disaster. But she gave me a look. A best-friend look. A "let me help you fix the mess you created even though I'm still angry at you" look. But I didn't want to take her up on it.

"You guys can't be here." I couldn't have Gabi and Cole near my parents. Under normal circumstances my parental units were more than a little scary. But today? They made Freddy Krueger and the Bride of Chucky seem like role models. I wasn't risking the souls of my favorite people. Regardless of how they'd acted the past few hours.

"I know you must be mad about before," Cole said. "I'm so sorry for what I said. I didn't me—"

"That's not it," I cut him off. "There's just a lot going on right now. You guys should go home."

"Not until we talk," Cole said. "I don't know why I keep doing these stupid things. It was like this anger just filled me."

"Cole, it's fine. I'm not mad. See?" I gave him a huge smile. "Now please, go home." On a normal day, I would have traded all my allowance just for the chance to hang out with Cole and hear him say how much he actually cared about me without being under the influence of powers. But not today. Today, I was worried about his soul. "You too, Gabi. Leave."

This time it was me sending her a look. One that said "I mean it, get lost, it's for your own good." I knew she understood the message, but she ignored it.

"We're not leaving you here," she said.

"Well, you should," I said, "after everything I did to you, you should want me to suffer."

Gabi put her hands on her hips. "You know me better than that. I'm always here for you—even when I'm mad. You need me now. I saw Reid walking around handing out gifts from his 'magic' bag. I know what's going on. We can deal with the Marc and Lance issues later."

She was a true-blue friend. I didn't deserve her. I couldn't put her in danger; I needed her to leave. Cole too. "It's not safe. You see the whacked-out stuff happening. Go home," I told them.

"Not without you," Cole said.

"I need to stay."

"Then so do we," Cole answered. Gabi nodded in agreement. Why did they have to be such good friends? I considered putting the hate spell back on them. But then they'd probably stick around just to spite me. "If it's really not safe, I'm not leaving you here."

I could feel my eyes tear up. Partially because it was nice to have someone . . . two someones . . . who cared so much about me. And partially because it scared me to have them so close to my father when he was on his evil power trip.

"And who do we have here?" Lou asked, sneaking up on us. "Did you bring me two new souls?"

"No," I said. "They don't want your wishes." I stood in front of my friends, blocking them from my father. But Cole kept moving, trying to get me to stand behind him.

"Sure they do," Lou said. "And I can use the pick-me-up after that Kristin mess." He looked right at Gabi. "What's your wish?"

"I don't want to make one," Gabi said. Her voice was wobbly. She recognized Lou. Even though he was a lot younger, he still had the same features.

"Let me guess," he said. "Popularity, boyfriend, fame, all of the above."

Gabi tugged at her braid. "Nothing."

Lou winked at her. "Think about it. I'll get back to you. What about you?" he said to Cole. Cole had met my father before. But he never would have suspected that Lou was the teenager standing in front of him.

"Cole, don't. It's a trick," I said.

Lou waved his hand, and I flew a few feet back. I stumbled and landed right on my butt. Fortunately that worked to my advantage because Cole ran to my side.

"Are you okay?" he asked, helping me out.

"No," I screamed. Not because my rear end hurt, but because Lou was bugging Gabi again to make a wish and sign her name on the waiver.

"What are you?" I screamed at Lou. "A genie? That's how you use your powers? To grant wishes? Seems totally beneath you. I thought you controlled

170

people. But now it seems like they're controlling you!"

Lou turned to face me.

Playing to his ego was actually working. "You're the devil. You don't need to waste your time here. At the stupid mall. You think that's what's going to impress Maggie? Relax. Take a vacation. I'm sure she'd like that better."

"You're right," he said.

Phew! He was buying what I said. While he took a break from *Sold Out* and relaxed in the sun, I could come up with a way to turn him back into his regular self.

"I *am* better than this," Lou continued. "I've been thinking way too small today. I don't know why I've been limiting myself to the *mall*." He sneered at the word. "It's time I took over the world!"

chapter

29

How come whenever I tried to make things better it had the opposite effect?

"Lou," I said, in the most soothing tone I could muster. "You don't want to take over the world. Talk about stress. Doesn't relaxing on a beach sound better? A tropical breeze. Sun shining. A hammock. Right, Maggie?" I called out to her. She wasn't paying attention. She was leaning up against the wall fixing her lip gloss. "Tell him. It beats working. Or school."

She glanced up from her compact mirror. "Huh?"

"Forget it," I said. She was no help.

"Powers equal stress," I told Lou. I could certainly vouch for that.

"You're wrong," he answered. "It's a gift. Who wants peace and tranquility when you can have destruction and chaos?!" Lou twirled his hand and pointed toward the side door of the mall. "Brace yourselves!" He laughed.

Suddenly it got dark outside. I could hear the wind rustling through the trees. And then it got worse. Shopping bags, mailboxes, and branches all got swept up. They were flying through the air.

Lou had created a twister, and I had a feeling none of us inside the mall would be heading to Oz. We'd be goners. And everyone who signed over their souls would go straight to the underworld.

That couldn't happen. I felt like the police commissioner on one of those cop dramas. The one who wouldn't let anyone get killed in their city. And this mall, this devil, was my beat.

I headed for the door.

Cole joined me. "Where are you going?"

"Just stay back."

"No," he said. "You can't go out there. Not now. Look at it."

"Trust me, Cole. I know what I'm doing."

He grabbed me, holding me tight.

"Let go," I cried.

"No, I'm not letting you out there."

I turned so I was facing him. Our eyes connected. He looked so concerned. Over me. I kissed him lightly on the lips. Just in case I didn't survive the twister, I wanted us to have one awesome last moment. And then with a flick of my wrist, I sent him sailing backward, right into Gabi. "Sorry," I whispered. But I was only doing what I had to do.

"Gabi!" I yelled. "Do *not* let him follow me."

I exited the mall. I tried to stay as close to the building as possible, hoping the wind wouldn't pick me up and send me flying. But the tornado was heading straight for me. I was definitely not in Kansas. I was in Hades. Hades on Earth.

It was getting closer. I could feel wind whipping my face and branches and debris slapping at my body. A rock or something hit me in the cheek. I closed my eyes and put out my hands to protect myself from any other flying objects. "No," I shouted, thrusting my arms straight in front of me.

And as I did, the wind simmered down.

I opened my eyes.

No way! My hands were keeping the tornado at bay. I guess it made sense. The twister was just like any other object I could control! I had been able to stop people and even a tidal wave in their tracks, so why not a twister?

I pushed it back a few feet farther from the mall. Then I focused on keeping it still.

I was doing it. But the bigger question was how long

would I be able to hold out? My arms were already getting tired. And it had only been a few minutes. How was I supposed to do this forever? Eventually I'd need sleep. After a day or two I was bound to doze off. And getting woken by a tornado pulverizing me was not exactly a dream come true.

It was getting harder and harder to keep the twister at bay. I took a look around. Behind me was the mall. Across the street was a grocery store. On either side were rows of houses. Anywhere I sent the tornado, I'd hurt someone.

My muscles were giving out. I needed to rest. To put my arms down. Down! Of course! I could bury the tornado in the ground.

With every ounce of energy I could muster, I forced the twister lower. It fought back, but I refused to give up. "Come on, upper-body strength," I whispered. So what if I had flunked the physical fitness test because I couldn't do a pull-up? I could still beat this force of nature. From pure will.

Mind over matter, I told myself. And it worked. Inch by inch the twister burrowed its way down. I could feel it pushing back against me, but I didn't let up. Not for a second. Not until the tornado was finally, completely gone.

I was completely spent. The energy was sucked out of me, but I still felt a slight rush fly through my body. I had done it! I stopped the twister from destroying the mall.

I totally deserved an A in gym class.

chapter

✧ 30 ✧

I breathed a sigh of relief as I went back in the mall. But I shouldn't have. Because my problems were far from over.

"You dare mess with me?" Lou's voice was low and hollow. It gave off an air of pure evil. I wasn't the only one who felt that way. A few in the crowd waiting for their wishes backed off. Not that they understood what had just happened. Just that they knew whatever it was wasn't good.

"Angel, get away from him," Cole called out.

"I'm fine, Cole. He won't hurt me. We're actually related," I admitted. "Just stay back." The words seemed to reassure Cole a little, but they didn't reassure me at all. I didn't know what Lou would do.

"I was just trying to stop anyone from getting hurt," I told Lou. "That's all."

His nostrils were flared. "You're no match for my

powers. You didn't like the tornado? How do you feel about this?" Lou snapped his fingers.

Suddenly, along with everyone else on that floor, I was hovering in the air, four feet off the ground. Then with a wave of his hand, Lou began spinning us like tops.

It felt like the musical express at Great Adventure. Only this ride didn't show any signs of stopping. Lou was turning all of us into mini-tornadoes.

"What's going on?" someone shouted.

"Just part of the documentary fun," Lou called back.

"Lou, let them go," I begged. "Please, do it for me, your little sister."

He sneered at me. "Do it yourself, if you can," he said. "You seem to love messing with my special gift. Let's see what you've got."

"I want to get down," one woman cried.

"Me too," several others echoed.

There were screams all around.

So I took Lou up on his offer. I tried to lower everyone using my powers. But it was hard to do while I was still spinning. My aim was off. Instead of sending them back to the ground, I caused them to collide into one another.

"Hmm," Lou said. "I guess you're no match for me."

"Maybe not. But I can try."

I grabbed onto Lou's shoulder to try and stop myself from spinning. Then I passed my hand up from the ground to the ceiling. I had powers, too. And this time they were spot on. I hit my target. My mother. And she went flying above the rest of the crowd.

She let out a scream. "Lou, get me down from here."

He did as he was told. The devil was under my mother's spell.

"I'm so sorry," he told her once she was back on the ground. "She'll pay for that."

Before he had a chance to live up to that promise, I sent a few people spinning in my mother's direction. She started screaming again.

"Lou, just knock it off," she yelled, covering her head with her hands. "Put them down already. It's not funny anymore. It's messing with my hair. That girl's shoe actually grazed my head. And their screaming is giving me a headache."

My mom's vanity paid off. In an instant, everyone was back on the ground.

"This is going to be one crazy documentary," Jaydin said, holding onto the wall to steady herself.

"I think I want out," Lana said. "This is freaky."

She could say that again.

179

chapter
✦ 31 ✦

Lana wasn't the only one who wanted out of Lou's wild ride. A lot of people were starting to leave. Finally, something was going right.

"Guess Lance is more powerful than you after all," Mom told Lou as more people vacated the area.

"He's nothing compared to me."

"Sure doesn't seem that way," she said.

Why did she have to goad him? Teen Mom was a nightmare.

"I'll get them back. You'll see," he said.

Lou was willing to do anything to prove to her how cool he was. He was smitten. "You love her," I said more to myself than to him.

"No, I don't," he said. But I was pretty sure he was lying. "I don't love anyone." He smiled again. "But in a second they're all going to love me! Better than love. They'll respect me. They'll worship me. They'll do whatever I want."

"What are you talking about?" I asked, even though I had a feeling I already knew.

"I'm going to cast a little spell—make the whole world go crazy over me. Then she'll see. Everyone will hand over their souls for nothing. It's perfect."

My heart was beating so fast, it felt like it was going fifty miles per hour on a treadmill. "You can't do that!"

"Actually, I can," he said.

This was all my mom's fault. He was doing this to impress her. Flirting was dangerous.

"Don't. You'll hate it. It's not fun having everyone chasing after you," I said. "Besides, you don't want the whole world to love you. You just want your family to love you. They're the people that care about you." I watched his face as I spoke. I hoped maybe I'd get through to him. That my words would trigger the old Lou. The Lou that said having a daughter was the most important thing in his life.

The new Lou didn't say anything. He just watched me. For half a second I thought I'd made a breakthrough.

I hoped it was recognition of the bond we had

shared. But it wasn't. It was a slow build to an evil laugh.

"Who needs a family's love, or anyone's love for that matter, when you can have adoration and servitude from the entire universe?!" he asked.

The answer was me. I needed my family's love. I didn't like having a snobby mother who didn't even know she was a mom and a dad who wanted to control the planet.

But in a few moments it wasn't going to matter. I was going to be under the devil's spell just like the rest of the world was about to be. I'd be his willing sidekick—ready to use my powers for whatever he wanted.

And then there'd be no one to stop him—or me.

chapter
✦ 32 ✦

I had to get away—somewhere where the devil's love spell wouldn't affect me. But that spot didn't exist. He was going to send his spell across the world.

Nothing was safe. There was nowhere to hide.

Gabi and Cole rushed over to me.

"How do you know that guy?" Cole asked me. "Is he for real?"

I nodded. "He is. That's why you have to go."

"I already told you," he said. "Not without you."

"Let me talk some sense into her," Gabi told him. "I can get her to come with us. Just give us a few minutes."

Cole hesitated, but finally agreed, leaving Gabi and me alone.

"You have to stop Lou," she said, looking around to make sure no one was listening. "I heard what he said. You need to fix this!"

"I don't know how!" I needed some sort of shield or some magical body armor—only I was clueless about how to create it. "I need more time."

"Lou," Gabi called out. "I changed my mind. I would like to make that wish now."

"What are you doing?" I shrieked.

"Buying you some extra time."

Buying it with her life. "Gabi, no," I pleaded.

"Yes," she said. "Trust me, Angel. I trust you. I know you'll figure something out."

Lou sauntered right up to Gabi. "Knew you'd come around. But I don't need you now. Pretty soon, you'll be begging me to take your soul. I won't even need to grant you a wish."

"I should have known you were all talk," she countered, her voice slightly shaking. "You probably don't know how to grant a wish, anyway."

"Of course I do."

"Yeah, right," she said. Gabi was taking a move straight from my playbook. Reverse psychology. He couldn't stand it when anyone doubted his abilities. "If you knew how, you would do it, instead of just talking about it."

"Fine," he said. "Make your stupid wish. What do you want?"

"First, tell me how this whole thing works again."

Tears were welling up in my eyes. Gabi was trying to stall Lou to give me a few extra minutes. If he figured out what she was up to, it'd be seriously dangerous for her. Worse than signing over her soul. Lou'd be out to get her.

I watched Gabi scrutinize the contract Lou handed her. There was only so long she could keep the devil waiting. I needed to get somewhere safe, somewhere I couldn't be affected by Lou's spell. I closed my eyes and focused. *Take me somewhere safe. Where I won't be in danger. Where I can still help!*

When I opened my eyes I was standing outside the backstage area where Lance and his mother were.

No!!!! What was I doing there? I needed to be somewhere safe, not the other side of the mall. And definitely not anywhere near Harmony Gold. The woman wanted nothing to do with me, and after the way she treated me, I wanted nothing to do with her, either. She wasn't going to help. It was just a waste of time. Time that I didn't have. Because while Gabi could talk more than anyone I knew, even she couldn't keep the devil distracted forever.

I jogged toward the exit of the mall. *Take me somewhere safe, take me somewhere safe, take me somewhere safe*, I commanded my powers. The next thing I knew I was being dragged back to the backstage door. It was like a magnet pulling me. I tried to fight it, but the force was too much.

"I said somewhere safe!" I took a few steps forward, but my body was thrust back against the door.

I tried again, but the same thing happened. My body kept smacking the entrance.

The thuds drew the attention of one of the guards. "Get away from there," he yelled.

Like I wasn't trying?!? Getting whacked against a piece of plywood was not exactly fun. I was sure to have a bunch of black-and-blues.

Somewhere safe, somewhere safe, somewhere safe! I kept thinking. But it didn't change my surroundings. I was still stuck there. Which wasn't only irritating me, but the guard, too.

He marched right over to me and tried to pull me away. Only he couldn't. The magnetic force was too strong. But that didn't stop him from trying. He yanked at my arms. I moved forward a few inches just to be whipped right back.

I felt like a yo-yo or a boomerang because no matter where I tried to go, I went ricocheting back to where I started from.

"How are you doing this?" he asked me as he continued to tug.

"I don't know." It was the truth. I wanted to get away from there as much as he did.

"Somewhere safe, somewhere safe," I said, not even caring that the guard heard. He was already completely confused. "Somewhere where Lou's spell won't affect me." But no matter how many times I said it, I wasn't budging.

The guard kept pulling at me with all his might. I actually got about ten feet away from the door. For three whole seconds. It was as if there were a magnetic pull between me (and now the guard) and the door.

The guard rubbed his head. He looked scared. "I don't know what you're up to or how you're pulling this off," he mumbled. "But I'm out of here." Then he just left me.

"Wait," I yelled after him. "You're supposed to be security. You need to help me." He didn't stop. I tried to follow him, but I just got sucked backward.

"Come on, powers," I muttered. "I need to be somewhere safe."

Not hanging *outside* of somewhere safe. Harmony Gold's protection shield would have been just the ticket. But, as we all know, it was created especially to keep me away. So there was no way I could get past the doors. I needed to find another safe haven. I turned my body around and tried to push myself away from the door. Bad move! I ended up getting thrust forward—headfirst.

I let out a huge grunt and tried again. Same result. I pounded at the door. "Stupid, stupid, stupid powers." But I wasn't about to give up. If I couldn't move forward and I couldn't move backward, I'd try moving to the side. With my body smashed against the wall, I shimmied to the right. I made it all the way to the corner, but the second I tried to step away from the wall, I was thrown back.

"Nooooooooooooooo!"

But my scream was met by laughter. Lots of it. Harmony Gold was practically convulsing with giggles.

"What are you doing here?" I asked, trying to peel myself away once again. The sight just made her laugh harder.

"I heard all the commotion and popped out to see what was going on." By *popped* she must have meant teleported. Because she definitely didn't use the door. That, I would have seen.

"What is going on," I said, "is that I'm trying to

get somewhere safe before Lou makes me and everyone else in the world worship him." I leaped forward, but mid-jump, I was pulled back. Now not only was I stuck to the door, but I was stuck to the door a foot off the ground. "Just great," I said, trying to kick my way down.

Harmony didn't even try to stifle her guffaws. "I haven't laughed this hard in ages."

"Glad I could help," I said, with as much sarcasm as I could. "Not that you would know anything about *helping*!" I tried to move again, but I was stuck like glue.

"All right, Angel," she said, taking my hand. "You win." The next thing I knew we were in the backstage area. She had teleported me!

"You wore me down," she said with a smile. "And the sight of you fighting with your powers . . ." She laughed again. "Well, let's just say I'd be a discredit to my angel race if I had ignored you."

Understatement.

"Wh-what is going on here?" Lance asked. I hadn't seen him standing there. Neither had his mom.

"I thought I told you to stay in the office!" she told him.

He was looking at us like we had appeared out of thin air—which we basically had. "This is crazy. How did you guys pop in here? And what is this about powers?" He rubbed his temples.

I had forgotten he didn't know the truth about himself. And Harmony had risked her secret for me. The least I could do was try and cover for her. "It was a magic trick. Pretty awesome, huh? I'd tell you how I did it, but we magicians take an oath. I'd get beheaded or something."

Harmony shook her head. "It's okay, Angel. There's no keeping the truth from him now. He's seen and heard too much today. It's time for him to know."

"Know what?" Lance asked.

"I'll explain it all in a minute," Harmony said to her son. "Let me just talk to her for a second. Angel and I have some unfinished business."

"But—," he objected.

"Trust me," she said.

I didn't blame him for wanting to know what was going on. I would have been demanding an answer if I were him. Lance didn't say anything, he also didn't move. He wanted to hear what his mom had to tell me. And she didn't make him leave.

"I guess maybe you don't have to be an adult to be ready for powers," she said. "Even though yours have obviously been acting up on you—you have been

190

trying to take responsibility," she said. "And I respect that. I was trying to bind Lance's powers. To keep him a regular human being for as long as possible. But I may have been wrong. You showed me that."

"Have you all lost your minds?" Lance asked.

His mother reached out and put her hand on his shoulder. "No, you'll understand everything soon." Lance looked like he was on a practical-joke show. Or like he thought his mom had accidentally sniffed some paint fumes.

"I promise," she said, "it will all make sense." Then she turned her attention back to me. "Now you have to get back out there. Clean up the mess you made."

"Don't make me go. You finally admitted I needed help. So help me. I can't go back out there. Lou's using a spell to make everyone adore him."

"I sensed that," Harmony said. "He sent the power across the globe. I can feel a surge like that. But it's over now. You can walk out there—you won't be affected."

"What are you guys talking about?" Lance asked. He looked like he needed a seat. Or maybe even a padded room.

"Angel," Harmony said. "It's time for you to go. I need to talk to my son."

"But what am I supposed to do? I tried to stop Lou, but I couldn't. I don't know how to fix this."

"Yes, you do," she said. "The way you got into this mess is the way you'll get out."

She didn't say anything else. And I didn't have a chance to. Before I could open my mouth, Harmony blinked her eyes, and I was back outside.

chapter
✧ 33 ✧

What was with that message? Talk about vague. I could get out of this mess the same way I got into it—what was that supposed to mean?

Was she telling me I needed to help Gabi? It had all started when I tried to get Lance to like her. But I had a feeling Harmony wouldn't be encouraging me to try to fix her son up. Maybe I just needed to get Gabi's soul back. But Harmony didn't even know that Gabi's soul was traded. I guess it was nice that she—and Gabi—believed I could fix everything, but I was having serious doubts. I was more clueless than ever.

I made my way back to Lou. There was a lot of noise coming from that direction. But the sound was nothing compared to the sight.

Lou had erected two huge chairs that he and my mother were perched on. It put them about ten feet higher than the crowd. My parents looked like the king and queen of the mall sitting there on their thrones. Especially since people were shouting about how they'd do anything for Lou and waving pieces of paper at him.

I nudged my way to Gabi and Cole. They didn't even notice me. Not until I grabbed the piece of paper from Cole's hand.

"Hey, I need that," he said. "I'm supposed to sign it and give it back."

"Do you even know who it's for? Who's asking you to do this?"

Cole looked at me like I had just asked him if he knew who Mara's Daughters were. "Yeah, only the greatest guy in the whole world. I hope he lets me be a part of his group. He's so cool. I want to work for him."

"No, you don't."

"Angel," Gabi interrupted. "It's okay. I felt just like you, but I came to my senses. Lou is amazing. I wish he was my dad." Gabi seemed to know all about Lou. All except that he was evil.

"Dad?" Cole asked. "He's practically our age."

"Umm, yeah, right," Gabi sputtered.

I didn't need to hear them talk about Lou anymore.

Or sing his praises. It was too much. I tore up Cole's contract.

"Whatcha do that for?" He immediately knelt down on the ground and tried to collect all of the tiny pieces.

"You'll thank me later."

He didn't even answer me, which was probably for the best. Cole did not look pleased at all. If he had opened his mouth, it probably would have been to dump me for ripping up his precious piece of paper.

I elbowed my way to the front of the crowd. I wasn't sure what I was going to do, but I hoped something would come to me.

"Lou," I yelled out.

"You're back," he said. "Come to tell me how much you adore me?"

"Not quite," I said. "Your little spell didn't work on me. I'm here to stop you."

"You're becoming quite the little pest." With a wave of his arm, Lou sent his admirers away from him. They crashed backward against the wall. But instead of being spooked, they were grateful. Grateful that the man they adored had touched them with his powers. He then jumped off his chair and stood right in front of me. He glared down at me, making me feel super-short. But I stared right back up at him.

195

"You know the best way to handle pests?" he asked me. "You squash them."

"And you know the best way to handle a power-obsessed devil?" I countered, channeling the fear and anger I felt into confidence. "You make everyone revolt against him."

"How about we start with her?" I said, pointing to my mom, who was staring at Lou like he was chocolate chip French toast with caramel syrup.

Stand up to Lou, don't do what he says, run from him and his evil ideas!

I concentrated on those thoughts until I saw Mom leap down from her chair.

Then she started sprinting. She darted down the hall, then back up, like she was doing laps. I hadn't meant to make her literally run! Was I ever going to get this power thing down?

Lou snapped his fingers and Mom was by his side.

"Maggie," he said.

But as he spoke, she covered her ears and started running again. It wasn't exactly what I was going for, but it worked. Mom wanted to get far away from Lou. So much so, that she ran to the end of the hall, rounded the corner, and took off out of sight.

I thought Lou would use his powers to stop her. To bring her back again.

But he didn't. He turned his focus to me. "You think you're clever? Well, you're not. I don't like being messed with. And I'm going to make you pay."

chapter

34

"Lou, calm down," I said. He meant business. His eyebrows furrowed. And his hands clenched into fists. Electric currents began to appear above them and took the form of energy balls. They hissed and sizzled and completely freaked me out.

"Pretty," someone in the crowd said. They didn't get it. He wasn't putting on a show. He was going to put a stop to me and my plan to save their souls.

"I warned you not to get in my way." Every step Lou took toward me, I took one back until I was up against the wall.

"Don't, Lou. We're related, remember? And I'm a lot more fun when I'm not barbecued."

The energy ball got bigger. My words weren't helping.

"You'd really do this?" I asked. "Here? In front of everyone?"

Lou shrugged his shoulders. He didn't care. Not about what anyone saw *or* what happened to his very own daughter. "I'm not going to cook you, I'm going to move you. Somewhere far, far away."

"Where?"

"I don't know," he said, studying the balls. "Maybe the desert, or an igloo in the middle of Alaska, or maybe I'll just make you the star of my very own fish tank."

He was really going to do it. He was really going to send me away. My breathing got extra fast. I couldn't help it. My whole body was heaving. I was terrified. Instead of feeling sorry for me, Lou laughed. "Don't feel so powerful now, do you?"

He tossed an energy ball higher in the air and caught it. It didn't hurt him, but I was pretty positive I wouldn't be so lucky. He tossed it up again. Then he sent it toward me, just inches above my head. It hit a lighting fixture. The thing disappeared. Was I next?!

I screamed, which was exactly the reaction Lou wanted. He laughed even harder. "Next one hits you."

There was nowhere to run. That teleporting trick sure would have come in handy. But it wasn't working. I couldn't make myself leave. I was stuck. About to be destroyed by my very own father. How could he do this? How could he not remember me? He said he loved me.

And then it hit me.

Love!

That's what Harmony was talking about when she told me to get out of this mess the same way I got in. Love was the answer. It got me into this mess, and it was going to get me out.

I could bet my soul on it.

chapter
35

"Say good-bye, Angel," Lou said, sending the energy ball into the air.

"Wait," I said. "If you get rid of me, you can't get my soul. I never signed a waiver or made a deal or anything. Give me one wish, and then you can do what you want."

"Why?" he asked.

"Because I want a final wish," I told him. "I deserve it."

Lou put the energy ball out. He rubbed his chin and didn't speak for a minute. "I won't allow a wish that will affect me. I'll deny it."

"Fine," I said.

"And you can't wish yourself out of this mess, either."

"All right." I knew it wasn't going to be that easy.

Lou wasn't stupid. He was just evil. "You can have final wish approval."

"I still don't get why you would want to sign your soul over to me. What's really going on?" He didn't trust me.

"I messed up some things and I want to fix my mistakes while I still can."

Lou snorted. "Trying to be all noble, are we, before you're banished from life as you know it?"

I wasn't trying to be noble at all. I was fighting for my life.

"What's the wish?" he asked.

"I used my powers a lot today, like when I made Mo—Maggie run away from you. I feel really badly about that. I know how much she liked you." I hoped Lou's feelings for my mom would cloud his judgment—make him grant my wish without realizing what I was really up to. "Look." I pointed as I saw her run past us again. Mom was still doing laps around the mall. "I can't leave her like that. Running for eternity. I want to undo it all. Any magic I used today, I want it gone. My soul for everything going back to the way it was before. Okay? Deal?"

He didn't say anything. Then a smirk crossed

his face. "Deal." Lou snapped his fingers and a piece of paper and a red pen appeared in his hand. "Sign here."

This was where faith came in. Faith that old Lou meant it when he said he loved me. Because I was about to sign over my soul to him. If he meant it, I'd get my soul back when this was all over. If not, there wouldn't be anything I could do. My destiny was in Hades.

chapter
✦✧36✧✦

As I crossed the last *T* in *Garrett*, a plume of smoke appeared and engulfed my parents. Right in front of my eyes, I watched them turn from teens to adults in a matter of seconds. Their faces thinned out and little creases formed. The gray in their hair returned and that cocky, defiant stance Mom had was replaced by a more rigid, in-control one. When it was all done, they looked old.

Thank goodness they were back.

I was ready for a happy, huggy family reunion. But it was going to have to wait. Because I kind of forgot that turning my parents into teens wasn't the only spell that needed to be reversed. I had buried a tornado into the ground. And since I had Lou reverse everything, that twister was emerging from below and heading straight for the mall.

The dust clouds were forming again and the wind was kicking up. I buried the thing once, I could do it again. If I could get to it before it crashed into the building.

I raced to the door. But the tornado was faster. I wasn't going to make it. The glass from the windows was going to shatter and fly straight at everyone in the room. I turned away to shield my face from any sharp shards. I waited and waited, bracing myself for the pain, but it never came.

Because with a twist of his hand, Lou made the tornado disappear. He didn't even have to go outside to do it.

"Thanks," I said.

The mass of people standing around applauded. I had forgotten they were there. Lou had forced them up against the wall, and they hadn't budged. They didn't dare disobey him. They worshipped him. They were still under the influence of his powers. It made no difference to them that he aged faster than a kid on a soap opera. He was their idol.

"Lou, that was brilliant," Mom said, moving closer to him. She actually hung onto his arm. "You are a remarkable man. But I've always known that."

Shoot. When my powers were undone, Mom no

longer felt the need to run away. But the powers Lou used on her, and everyone else, were still fully intact. If he didn't fix her, I was totally going to make her bolt again. Because watching my mother fawn over Lou, or anyone for that matter, was icky. "You're going to put her back to normal, aren't you?"

He hesitated for a second. He seemed to like having her there. "Yes." Lou waved his hand over her head.

Mom let go of him superfast.

"Welcome back," I said and plastered a smile on my face. I wasn't sure if they'd be angry because of the problems I caused or proud of the way I handled them.

"We have some serious talking to do," my mother said. She was shaking her head, and the look she was giving me accentuated the crease in her forehead. The one that wasn't there when she was a teen. Whoa! Did worrying about me cause Mom's wrinkles? It would explain why she liked to punish me all the time. Payback!

Great. She was angry. She could have at least thanked me for my brilliance in figuring out how to make her an adult again. She sure seemed to like acting like one. She was already bossing me around.

"You're in serious trouble, young lady," Lou said.

"I've warned you about using advanced powers without supervision."

Like I did it on purpose. I couldn't believe he was punishing me. Hello! I just saved the world—from him. He was probably just embarrassed that my powers worked on him. "It was an accident."

"We'll talk about this at home."

Why did I forget to add a clause to my wish? That my parents wouldn't remember any of my stupid moves! That would have saved me a lot of trouble. Instead they remembered everything. Just perfect.

Lou didn't even look happy to see me. If he had been, he would have apologized that he didn't recognize me before and threatened to throw energy balls at me. But nope. He just wanted to look all tough in front of Mom. He probably didn't even care about me at all.

"Let me guess," I said. "I bet you're going to keep my soul so you can control me from now on." Lou took a deep breath. But he didn't deny it.

"What!?" Mom said.

I waited for Lou to say something. To prove me wrong, but he didn't. I couldn't even think straight anymore, I was so upset. "That's right," I said to Mom. "While you were all busy paying attention to how good your hair looked and how cute your boyfriend was, Lou was taking my soul." I turned back to him. "That's all you ever wanted from me, anyway, wasn't it?"

Lou looked down at the paper. He took another deep breath. "I don't want your soul, Angel. I want you to be safe. You're my daughter. You could have gotten yourself hurt or worse. Just thinking about that makes me . . ."

He stopped speaking and looked up toward the sky. Was he fighting back tears? Over me?

"You didn't act like you were worried about me," I said, "Not when you were telling Mom about all my powers this morning."

Lou crumpled up the piece of paper that held the rights to my soul tightly in his fist. "I was doing that to protect you. You see what can happen when your powers go out of control. You need your mother. Keeping that kind of secret from her obviously affects your emotions. Look what happened today. I almost hurt you. And I couldn't have lived with myself knowing that I had done that," he said, staring right at me with a crazy intense look. "Thankfully it didn't come to that."

He threw the paper ball to the ground and it burst

into flames. I watched as the fire fizzled out. I felt a sense of relief as I looked at the pile of ash. My contract was null and void. My soul was mine again.

"You mean everything to me, Angel," he said. "Do not scare me like that again."

Scare him? He was the one who had been terrifying. But as I studied his face, I realized that was exactly the point. Lou wasn't mad at me because I had used my powers. He was mad at me because I put my life in danger. Mad that he almost hurt me. Mad that he couldn't protect me.

He did care about me. For the first time in my life, I knew what it felt like to have a father who worried about me. I moved in closer to him. He held out his arms and I fell into them, and then he wrapped me in a big bear hug as the tears fell down my cheeks.

The devil loved his daughter after all.

chapter
✦ 37 ✦

"I want in on this, too," Mom said. She reached out for a hug. "I'm glad you're safe," she said, pulling me into her so tightly she almost squeezed my breakfast out of me.

"Me too," I agreed, hugging her back.

"But this doesn't mean you're off the hook," she warned. Of course it didn't. Mom was the punishment queen. But having a strict mom sure beat having one that didn't care. "You still have a lot of answering to do."

What was sure to be a lecture from Mom was interrupted by a tap on my shoulder. It was Gabi. "Can you get your dad to pose for a picture with me?" she whispered.

"What? Why?" I asked.

"Because he's *Lou*—the all-powerful, the all-wonderful, the all-spectacular."

Ugh. Lou had taken the love spell off of Mom, but everyone else in the mall—and the world—was still under it. I looked around. The crowd was watching us intently. Only they were too afraid to get close and risk upsetting Lou. "Not now, Gabi."

"Come on, please! I thought you were my best friend. You owe me."

"Fine, you can have a picture," I said. Lou posed next to Gabi.

"Looks like I have a little bit of fixing up to do here," he said.

"No kidding," I said, pointing to the MAKE A WISH sign emblazoned in fire and all his adoring fans staring eagerly at him.

Lou shook his head. "Maybe more than a *little* cleanup. This is going to take more than a wave of my hand. Let me send you and your mother back home. I'll meet up with you afterward."

"Wait," I said. "I have some fixing up of my own to do. Can I stay?"

They agreed. So as Lou got to work on his problems, I got to work on mine.

I went to go see Lance and his mother.

The guard that had tried to pull me away from the door was still there. This time I didn't fling him away. I

211

had a better, non-power related solution to get by him without any trouble. "Lou sent me," I said. Just like Gabi and ninety-nine percent of the world, the guard was under the love spell.

"Lou?!" he said. "You saw him? Is he here?"

"Yep, he's right down that way. By the Apple store."

He rushed off before I even finished the sentence, leaving me unattended. I knocked on the door. "Lance, Harmony, can I come in, please?"

The door swung open and I went inside.

Harmony was standing a few feet away. "It's over," I said. "Lou is back to normal."

"I know," she answered. "I could sense it. But I'm not surprised. I knew you'd figure out the answer. I knew you didn't need my help."

That made one of us. She had taken a big risk there. I wouldn't have counted on a thirteen-year-old with whacked-out powers to save the planet. But I guess angels have more faith in us than we do. "Thanks," I said.

"No," she said, actually smiling at me for once. "I think I owe you the thank you. Both for fixing the Lou problem and for helping me realize that Lance was ready for his powers."

I felt like I had my own little halo sitting on my head.

Not just because someone finally acknowledged that I had done something good, but because she believed in me. An angel believed in me. Maybe Harmony wasn't so bad after all.

"Is Lance around?" I asked.

She called to him. As he entered the room, he looked calmer and more peaceful than I had ever seen him. Although it could have been because I wasn't banging down his door for once.

I wasn't quite sure what to say. I had turned his life upside down. "I'm so sorry for dragging you into my mess."

"It's okay," he said. "Really."

"I'm sorry you had to find out you were an angel that way."

He shrugged a shoulder. "I'm happy to know my real identity. I always felt like I was different."

"Well, you are, like, the biggest star around," I said. That in itself made him way different than most people.

"Yeah, but this is bigger. This is way cooler." His face looked almost angelic, if that was possible.

"So what are you going to do?"

"Head back to Hollywood. There are a lot of messed-up people there who could use my help," he said.

"Sure you don't want to stay? That girl Gabi I was

telling you about is worth moving to Pennsylvania for. And she'd make an awesome girlfriend."

"Angel," he said and shook his head.

I glanced at the floor. Hey, I had to try. "Well, you're not giving up acting, are you?" If he did, then Gabi would really be upset. Along with most of America and TV executives everywhere.

"Nope. It'll help me reach more people."

Wow. Hot, famous, and an angel. He was quite the triple threat.

"Well, thanks again," I said and headed for the door. "Oh, one more thing," I said turning back. I flashed Lance a big, dimple-filled smile. "Any chance I can get an autograph?"

chapter 38

"I thought you might be here," Lou said as I exited the backstage area. "Spell reversed, souls returned, wishes taken back."

I just nodded. I wasn't quite sure what to say to him. I had written Lou out of my life not too long ago. He broke a promise—lost my trust. And until I knew for sure he was over his wicked ways for good, I said I wanted no part of him. Sure, he made some progress today undoing the contracts he made—including mine. But what if tomorrow he slipped back? Reverted to old . . . I mean, *young* Lou? And how was I to know if he really returned all the souls he'd bought at the mall? "Every single one?"

"Yes." He looked convincing, but he was the devil. He'd win the Olympic gold for lying.

"How did you convince them to give back what

they got?" I remembered that when I granted Gabi her unlimited wishes, I couldn't force her to give them up. She had to do it freely. It was part of the deal.

"I can be pretty persuasive when I want to be."

My eyes got wide. What did that mean? Did he threaten them with an energy ball?

"Relax," Lou said, looking at my face. "I just made sure I asked to undo the wishes before I took off the adoration spell. They were happy to oblige. Anything for their hero."

Lou laughed at that.

I didn't. After today, I never wanted to hear about spells again. The thought alone made me cringe. "You didn't leave any of them worshipping you, did you?"

"Would I do that?"

I crossed my arms. That was the point—I didn't know *what* Lou would do.

He shook his head. "No, I didn't leave them like that. Everyone is back to normal."

"Yeah," I snorted. "Except that they saw a man do impossible things like stop a tornado and send them flying in the air and watch themselves fall in and out of love with a stranger faster than the contestants on *The Bachelor*."

"Well," he said, his mouth moving in a half grin, "I may have taken care of that, too."

"May have?" That did not sound good. "What did you do?"

"I played around with their memories."

"But that's dangerous! You're always telling me erasing people's minds could have serious consequences."

"So could having them remember what they saw," he said. "But I didn't erase their memories. I made them fuzzy. And just the parts that had to do with powers. They think they saw a magic show but can't remember all the details."

"Are they going to be okay?"

"They're going to be just fine."

I had to take his word for it. And truthfully, I was relieved. I didn't want my secret out. Not to anyone. But especially not to Cole. And I didn't need him to remember hating me or even being crazy obsessed. Although I was going to keep a few of those voicemails he sent!

"Shall we go home?" Lou asked.

chapter
✦ 39 ✦

As Lou and I headed for the exit, we walked by D.L., who was still in the security area. I had almost forgotten about him. Lou and all his talk about undoing the wishes and whatnot distracted me.

"Wait," I said. "D.L. is in trouble because of me. He wouldn't be in there if he hadn't helped me try and fix the mess I made. I have to get him out."

Lou shook his head as he sized up the guard. "I don't think they'll listen to a thirteen-year-old."

"They have to! He can't stay in there."

"You didn't let me finish," Lou said. "They won't listen to a thirteen-year-old, but they'll listen to me. I'll get him out."

I watched as Lou spoke to the guard. I don't know what he said, but it worked! The guard gestured for D.L. to get up.

But instead of just letting him go, Lou pulled D.L. aside. It made me nervous. What did he want with him? I ran up to the two of them and interrupted their conversation.

"Hey," I said. "Everything okay here?"

"Everything's just fine," Lou said.

But I wasn't talking to him, I was talking to D.L. I wanted to hear it from him. "Lou, can you give us a few minutes?" I asked.

He nodded and stepped away.

"You all right?" I asked. I eyed D.L., looking for any signs that Lou may have messed with his memory or tried to recruit him for demon duty. But he looked the same as usual.

"Yeah," he said.

I needed to know for sure that his soul was safe. "What did Lou want?"

"He just introduced himself and told—"

"Introduced himself? Who did he say he was?"

D.L. raised an eyebrow at me. "He told me he was your father. What did you think he was going to say?"

"Nothing," I said and tried my best to smile. "Did he say anything else?"

"Just told me to stay out of trouble."

"That's it?" I questioned.

I could feel D.L. studying me. "What's going on?" he asked.

"Nothing. I'm just being dumb. Anyway, I'm sorry I got you in trouble," I said.

He ran his hand through his hair. "I'm used to it. Besides, nothing happened other than wasting a day sitting here. They never got through to my parents."

That was a relief. "Well," I told him, "one other thing happened." I held up a picture of Lance. "I got you this."

"Just what I always wanted," he said, the sarcasm dripping off every word.

"Look at it closer," I said, swatting the picture at him.

"'To the world's most beautiful girl and a rising star. Look forward to working with you one day. Love, Lance.'" I had come up with the wording myself. I knew Courtney would flip when she saw it. I hated her, but I owed it to D.L.

"You did it!" he said. "I didn't think you'd pull it off, Garrett."

"I guess you just need a little more faith," I said.

"Angel," a voice called out.

I turned around to see Cole and Gabi headed for me.

"What's going on?" Cole asked, looking back and forth between me and D.L. He was biting his lip and looked a little uncomfortable.

"Nothing," I said. "Where were you two?" I said, turning the question back onto him. I tried to block out the image of them listening to a romantic song together. "What were you guys up to?"

"Honestly," he said, shifting back on his feet. "I'm not quite sure. This whole day is kind of muddy." Cole pulled out a CD. It was the new Mara's Daughters single. "But I do remember getting you this. The name made me think of you." He didn't look at me as he handed it over.

My skin went all tingly. "Thank you so much!" The song was called "Beautiful Wonder."

He smiled at me. One of those great, lopsided smiles. "Gabi told me you didn't have it yet."

So that's what they had been doing at the music store . . . picking out something for me! It really was time for me to stop suspecting everyone around me. I was always wrong! "It's weird," Cole said. "Some things I remember, and others are so hazy."

"Yeah," Gabi added, giving me a look like she knew I had something to do with her memory lapse. "It's a blur."

221

"Really?!" I asked. Maybe Gabi forgot all the stuff I said about her to Lance and Marc. "So you don't remember waiting to see Lance or what happened before that?"

"No, all of that is burned into my memory," she said.

Figured. The spell stuff didn't happen until after I humiliated her. I took Gabi's arm and pulled her away from Cole, D.L., and my dad.

"Are you mad at me?" I asked her.

"Well, I'm not exactly happy."

"I'm so sorry, Gabi. I'm going to make it up to you. I know it didn't work with Marc or Lance, but I'll find you someone."

"Angel!" Gabi threw her hands in the air. "Don't you see? I don't want your help."

"But don't you want a boyfriend?"

"Of course I do," she said. "But not like that. Not because you use your powers or beg someone to go out with me. I want them to *really* like me. Because of *me*."

"I totally get it," I said. And I really did. Having all those people wanting to hang out with me just because of a love spell wasn't fun at all. "I won't try to make a match where there isn't one. But I *was* just trying to help, you know."

"I know." She linked arms with me and we walked back to the group. We were going to be just fine.

"Want to grab some ice cream?" Cole asked Gabi and me.

"Definitely," I said. "I'm starving." One mouthful of vanilla soft serve earlier in the day was definitely not enough.

Lou cleared his throat. "We need to get going."

"But Lou—"

"Angel," he said in a no-nonsense voice.

"Fine. Sorry, guys," I said.

We said our good-byes. I thought Cole was going to kiss me, but he looked at my father and gave me a fist bump instead. A fist bump!?

"You want to come with us?" Gabi asked D.L. before she headed off with my boyfriend.

"Yeah, why not?" he said, and gave her a smile. One of his melty ones.

"No way," Gabi said, looking at what he was holding. "You got an autograph? I'm jealous."

D.L. looked from the photo to Gabi. "You can have it," he said and handed it to her.

"Really?" she asked. I was thinking the same thing.

"Yeah," D.L. said. He looked back at me and shrugged his shoulders.

Maybe what I said to D.L. before hit home. Maybe he was ready to give pretty *and* nice a try. How cool would that be? Courtney would flip!

"Let's go, Angel," Lou said.

"Coming," I said as I watched my friends walk off. I couldn't help but notice Gabi giving D.L. a shy smile. It looked like I wasn't going to be the only one with a juicy story to tell.

chapter

Mom bit at her nails as Lou filled her in on what she missed. Mom never bit her nails. She even yelled at me when I did it. That couldn't have been a good sign.

I dropped down in the big Buddha chair, but it couldn't protect me. My parents were prepared for punishment.

I thought about reminding them that this was how we got in the mess in the first place, that if they had just understood what it was like to be younger, I never would have accidentally turned them into teens. But I bit my tongue. Chances were that would just make them angrier.

Mom studied my face. "I can't believe you didn't feel you could tell me about your powers."

Really? She shouldn't have been so stunned. She

totally freaked out when Lou told her the truth this morning. Why would I have wanted to go through that? "I didn't want to get you upset."

"I wouldn't have been."

I didn't say "yeah, right," but apparently the look on my face did.

"It's true," Mom said. "It's not the powers that bother me. I'm making potions and protection spells all the time. Your gift is just a little stronger." I hadn't thought about that. Mom was fascinated with otherworldly things—especially powerful, life-altering ones. She might have actually thought what I could do was cool.

"But," she said. Ahh. I should have known there'd be a *but*. "It's how you used your powers that bothered me."

"Excuse me?" I had been ready for this one. I knew she'd say something about how I wasn't responsible. "This from the woman who wanted to use powers to get back at her old 'friend' Kristin? Is that how I'm supposed to use my special gift? For revenge?"

Pretty sure I saw Lou stifle a laugh. One point—Angel.

"Is Kristin okay?" Mom said, turning to Lou. "I completely forgot about bringing her to the mall."

"She's fine," Lou said. "I took care of everything."

Mom let out a little breath. "I was under some sort of spell," she told me. "Otherwise I would *not* have done that."

"The spell only turned you back into a teen and made you understand powers. It didn't mess with your younger self's morals," I argued.

"You can't hold me accountable for what I did," she said. "I was only a kid."

"And so am I! If that's the case, then you can't hold me accountable, either!"

"It's not the same thing, Angel," Mom said. But it certainly sounded like the same thing to me. "I was very different when I was younger."

"No kidding."

Mom lowered her head a little. "I had a lot of growing up to do. I'm not proud of the way I acted back then, but people change. I changed. But this isn't about me, it's about you."

"Oh, I see," I said, crossing my arms. "You could do whatever you wanted when you were a teen. But me? One little thing and I'm grounded for life."

"Believe me," Mom said. "I got my share of punishments, too, and I didn't think I deserved them, either. But I did."

She wasn't letting me out of this.

"But," she said, with a surprising lilt to her voice, which gave me a little bit of hope. "Powers are a big responsibility. One you need training in so they don't accidentally go off and you don't cause any more accidents. So maybe if you actively work on controlling them and promise not to try anything advanced without supervision, we can let this go—this time."

Yes! I was off the hook. I was feeling awesome until I saw Mom look at Lou. Her lips curled up into a little smile. And her eyes were sparkling. No way! Even without the adoration spell, my mom was still crushing on him. Hadn't she learned her lesson all those years ago? Yeah, Lou had his moments. But you could NOT trust the devil. Especially with your heart. Maybe Harmony knew a nice angel she could hook my mother up with. There was no way I'd let Mom get back together with Lou again. Talk about disaster.

"Sounds like a plan to me," Lou said, catching my mother's eyes.

This was bad.

"Fine." I stood up, trying to direct the attention to me. "If I agree, then am I in the clear?"

"You also have to promise not to use your powers for any more personal gain, like to play cupid."

"Promise," I told her. But I had my fingers and toes crossed, so it didn't really count. Because let's be honest, there was no chance I'd be able to do that. Especially not when I had Gabi and D.L. to think about. Their romance might need a teeny push from me. After all, I had only promised Gabi not to make a match where there wasn't one. And there was clearly something going on between her and D.L. "Now can I go?"

"Not so fast," Lou said.

Shoot. Had he seen my fingers? Or was he just trying to spend more time around my mother? Neither was good.

"What?" I asked cautiously.

"I just want you to know I'm glad you're safe. You're the most important thing to me, Angel. I love you."

I just stood there. I felt tears forming in the back of my eyes. It was nice having him back in my life, but what if he did something evil again? What if he didn't mean all the things he said? It was too risky to let him into my life.

Mom interrupted the silence. "Why don't you stay for dinner, Lou?"

He looked at me, waiting for my approval. I

shrugged my shoulders. I guess he could stay if he wanted to.

"I'll barbecue," he said, making a little flame appear in the air. "It is my specialty."

"Perfect," Mom said, pulling some vegetables and chicken out of the fridge.

Lou grabbed the ingredients and began to juggle a few tomatoes.

But Mom wasn't watching where she was going and walked right into the path of Lou's flying salad. I couldn't help but laugh as a tomato nailed her in the head. She picked up a pepper and threw it at Lou. Then they both looked at me, and baby carrots started coming my way. I ducked for cover.

For a second we actually felt like a real family. A real, messed up family, but a family all the same.

I looked at Lou. Maybe Mom was right. Maybe people really could change.

And while I didn't necessarily like everything my father did, I knew he was trying and that I loved him.

And for now, that was enough.

Shani Petroff is a writer living in New York City. *Bedeviled: Love Struck* is the fourth book in the Bedeviled series. She also writes for news programs and several other venues. When she's not locked in her apartment typing away, she spends a whole lot of time on books, boys, TV, daydreaming, and shopping online. She'd love for you to come visit her at www.shanipetroff.com.

Be on the lookout for . . .

Hello, Gorgeous!

Blowout

Mickey thought she was
hired to sweep up all the hair.
What she hadn't bargained for
was picking up all the dirt . . .

CHAPTER 1

"Countdown to gorgeous!" cheered Megan as she passed me in the salon chair on her way to the back room. Megan, a college student with cascading blond hair and full, pink cheeks, was the receptionist at Hello, Gorgeous!, which happens to be my mom's salon and one of my very favorite places to be in the entire world. It was Sunday—my thirteenth birthday—and the salon wasn't open yet. Everyone was here special, just for me.

For as long as I can remember, my birthday presents have centered around hair. It started with my Barbie Princess Styling Head when I was four. I thought it was the greatest present ever invented. From the moment I got Barbie's head out of the box, I brushed, braided, curled, and clipped her hair within an inch of her princess-head life.

For my tenth birthday, my parents kicked it up

"Countdown to gorgeous!" cheered Megan as she passed me in the salon chair on her way to the back room. Megan, a college student with cascading blond hair and full, pink cheeks, was the receptionist at Hello, Gorgeous!, which happens to be my mom's salon and one of my very favorite places to be in the entire world. It was Sunday—my thirteenth birthday—and the salon wasn't open yet. Everyone was here special, just for me.

For as long as I can remember, my birthday presents have centered around hair. It started with my Barbie Princess Styling Head when I was four. I thought it was the greatest present ever invented. From the moment I got Barbie's head out of the box, I brushed, braided, curled, and clipped her hair within an inch of her princess-head life.

For my tenth birthday, my parents kicked it up a notch when they surprised me with a smoky blue vanity desk with a three-way mirror. It came complete with matching containers filled with new brushes, combs, and clips. That's when I started styling my *own* head within an inch of its frizz-filled life. Still haven't had much luck there.

Last year, for my twelfth birthday, I got an actual styling chair for my bedroom, which gave my room more of a beauty-zone feel. It doesn't have the hydraulics to pump up and down, but it's exactly like something you'd see in a real salon: black with a silver footrest and everything. I tried getting my best friend/next-door neighbor, Jonah, to sit in it so I could tame his cowlick, but he said he'd rather jam bobby pins up his nose than play hair salon with me.

But this year I finally received the best, most amazing birthday present ever. After a dinner at my favorite brick-oven pizza place last night with Mom and Dad, today I got my real birthday present—I became an official employee at Hello, Gorgeous!

Well, *part-time* (Saturday, Sunday, and Wednesday after school) official employee, but still. Mom had finally, after years of my begging, pleading, and tantrum-throwing, agreed to let me work as a sweeper at her über-successful salon. She was even going to pay me, though I totally would have done it for free. Mom went on and on about how it was a trial run and if I slacked off at the salon—or at school (Rockford Middle School)—I'd have to go. Which was never going to happen. I'd been waiting too long to be a part of the salon team, and the last thing I wanted to do was disappoint my mom. I wanted her to be proud of me and see that I had style-sense in my genes, too.

But my longing to work at Hello, Gorgeous! wasn't only about hair. I secretly hoped that working at a salon would give me some of the spark that all the stylists there seemed to have. You know, that sass that enabled them to say whatever was on their minds, in front of anyone, whenever it popped into their heads. I needed some of that. I'd been so painfully shy most of my life that I wouldn't even play Telephone with the kids in first grade. But unless I wanted Jonah to be my only friend for the rest of my life, I had to come out of my turtlelike shell. It was a must.

"How about some loose curls?" asked Violet. She was the store manager and most-talented stylist, and because of that she had the second-most prestigious station in the salon, second from the entrance, right behind my mother's. Not only was it my first day, but I was also getting a mini makeover as part of my birthday present.

When I came into Hello, Gorgeous! this morning with Mom, the salon had been dark and quiet until I flipped on the light in the break room, where practically half the staff jumped up and yelled "Surprise!" I nearly fainted, but when I saw the doughnuts they'd bought and the two signs they'd hung—HAPPY BIRTHDAY, MICKEY! and WELCOME, GORGEOUS!—I knew it was going to be the most epic day of my life so far.